It'
C(
th
co

keeps the cowboy coming back to his clown for satisfaction and relief. Brightie feels filled and satisfied despite the pain and suffering he endures.

The two are the perfect pair until Cody's darkest
secrets threaten to tear them apart.

Rodeo is the toughest sport. It's savagely violent; even
the clowns are made of steel. The cowboys are strong,
deep, and brutal in bed. Brightie must adapt to the
cowboy life or perish.

CONFESSIONS OF A RODEO CLOWN

PETER SCHUTES

*To Jacob
Ride that bull...
then wash your
hands*

Peter Schutes

Confessions of a Rodeo Clown
Copyright © 2018 by Peter Schutes Publishing.
Pulp Edition © 2024
All rights reserved.

ISBN: 978-1-963667-01-1

Cover Illustration by Duncan MacLeod

This book is for ADULT AUDIENCES ONLY. It contains
substantial sexually explicit scenes with multiple partners and graphic
language which may be considered offensive by some readers.

All sexual activity in this work is consensual and all sexually active
characters are 18 years of age or older.

CONTENTS

❧ I ❧

CODY

It was the Clinton Firemen's Rodeo where I first laid eyes on Cody Cameron. He was the biggest fellow I ever seen that rode the bulls. He was 6'4" and musta weighed about 250 pounds. He was built like a brick shithouse. He couldn't see me smiling at him from the barrel in my clownface makeup. All he could see was the massive steer between his legs, bucking and throwing him now left, now right. He placed second that day with 78 points. Some tall, thin cowboy from Georgia beat him out.

After his ride, I went back to the lockers to re-apply my makeup. I was hoping to catch a glimpse of him, but he was gone. I didn't know why I felt sad. I didn't know much of anything. It was a cold, empty feeling in my chest.

I was a late bloomer. All my buddies back at Clinton High had girls their senior year, but I just stood on the sidelines and watched. That year, Bill Gresham, the toughest cowboy at school, took me out behind the gym down by the crick.

He asked me, "Brightie, when you gonna get yourself a girl"?

"Don't know, jus' waitin', I guess."

"See how you are"? He winked at me. Then he put his arm around my middle, pounded me on top of my head, and laughed. That was the first time I felt hollow inside after he walked away. And now, two years later, here I was at the rodeo, hiding from the bull in my blue barrel, a big frown painted on my face, hiding that hollowness inside, as empty as that barrel when I climbed out after the tall, thin cowboy from Georgia won the round.

I guess someone was watching over me because about four months later, they asked me to be Second Clown in Laramie at the Mountain States Circuit Finals.

I hadn't ever been out of Oklahoma except for a field trip to Amarillo. I wasn't so sure I should go. But Bill Gresham heard about it, and he was downright envious, so that cinched it for me. I decided to go. They was even gonna pay my motel room and everything. I sleep in a room with my two little brothers. This was gonna be my first time ever in a room by myself.

They even paid my bus fare. I just had to wear a pair of overalls with a gigantic Little Debbie Snack Cake logo on 'em. They even gave me a locker in the locker room!

My momma packed my dinner for the bus ride. She smoothed down my hair and says, "Brightie, I want you to come home with some stories to tell."

I says, "Yes'm," kissed her cheek, grabbed my dinner sack, put it in my sports bag full of clown gear, and headed off to the bus station. I'd never noticed the bus depot in Clinton before. It was full of the strangest folks, not like you see in church. My bus ticket was waiting there at the window, just like they said. I had to pee real bad. The men's room was nothing but a lot of cowboys playing with their dicks at the urinal. I got hard and had to piss through my boner. It hurt to high hell.

When we got to Laramie, I was so glad to be able to stretch my legs. I had tried to sleep on the bus, but my head was so full of worries I couldn't keep my eyes closed. The motel was next to the bus depot. After I found my room, I laid my stuff down and went for a Coke from the vending machine. That's when I noticed him standing at the end of the hallway.

Cody Cameron seemed bigger when he wasn't riding a giant bull. They musta had to custom-make his jeans. The legs was big around as tree trunks and skin tight, nearly busting the seams. He sure wasn't no clown like me. He had on a sky blue shirt with real pearl snaps and a silk neckerchief. His eyes was hid under his black ten-gallon hat, but I could still see him watching me like a cat eying a canary. His hands were on his hips; he had a wedding ring. He had an extra cowboy hat rolled up and shoved deep in his pocket; I found out later it wasn't a hat, and it wasn't in his pocket neither.

There it was again, that sad emptiness out of nowhere. I didn't have a name for it, except maybe lonesome. I turned to go.

"Hey, boy!"

I turned back real sheepish.

"You're a clown, aintcha"?

"Yessir."

Then he walked away. My eyes stung, and I wished I was back home, eating momma's cooking.

When he got to his door, he says, "Well, you better keep that bull off my ass, or you're gonna be one sorry clown." He tipped his hat like a gentleman, but he wasn't smiling.

I ran back to my room and slammed the door hard. I stripped naked to take my bath; I discovered they didn't have a tub, just a dirty shower full of tiny bars of Lifebuoy soap. I'm not proud to say that I cried right then. I was so tired; I just wanted to soak my bones in a tub, and instead, I was going to have to stand there. So

I skipped it and flopped face first into my pillow, naked as the day I was born.

❧ 2 ❧
TOILET TEASE

The next thing I knew, it was morning. Everyone was running to the Cracker Barrel because that was where they were paying for our breakfast.

For most of the rodeo, I just stood around as a backup. They didn't need clowns for horses or steer roping. The overalls was real loose, so's they was more like a denim dress. I looked pretty silly, but those overalls were buying my breakfast, so I just kept quiet and pretended I always dressed this bad.

Underneath I had on these tight red stretchy long johns. They was chafing and itching, so I went to the bathroom to fix the situation. I didn't want a rash. It was still bareback bronco riding; the bulls weren't for another hour at least.

That's when I saw him again. He was taking a piss when I came in. His pants were down real low, and his big ass was showing. It was rounder than you see on those tall, skinny cowboys. He turned over his shoulder and smiled. I figured he was done pissing, but he still just stood there. I was waiting for him to leave so I could get my long johns off in private, but he wasn't leaving. I brushed past him to go in a toilet stall, and I realized why he was still there, shaking out the piss. He

5

musta been part bull because even soft, his pecker was thick as a Coke can and twice as long. That wasn't a hat in his front pocket last night. His balls were big, but his fat dick made them seem smaller. He was so big he had to lower his jeans so he could take it out or stuff it back in his BVDs. He couldn't use a fly like regular folks; it would never fit through the opening.

A rush of blood went from my stomach down between my legs. My pecker was getting hard. Then I realized he could see me staring at his bull dick. He grinned and winked at me before wadding it up and stuffing it back into his undershorts. He hitched his pants back up over his big round butt. Then he walked out of the bathroom, whistling a tune. He turned and gave me a smile before he stepped out into the arena.

Then that empty sadness set on real bad. I forgot why I was in the bathroom and just left the long johns chafing my crotch and balls. My rock-hard dick was hidden inside the folds of the giant overalls. I was beet red under my white clown makeup. Hiding in plain sight, I was figuring out what that sadness really meant, but it was soon time to work because bull riding was about to start.

FIGHTING BULLS

The guy doing First Clown was a plumb idiot. He didn't care if the new riders made it out alive or not. One young Mexican guy got smacked in the side of the head and lost some teeth because that damn clown was being a ham and forgot to pay attention. Darrel, the clown in the barrel, rolled his eyes; I could see he thought the same.

Once the amateurs were done, it was time for the 99s. We called them that because 99 percent of the cowboys who climbed onto these bulls got thrown off before the eight-second mark.

Cody was a weekend cowboy, not a champion. He had just a few wins under his belt and a career total of 8,000 dollars. He was up against some real big names. These were champions with a lot of wins and a lot of money. They were just riding here to keep their standing and earn fast money. They didn't love the rodeo. But they were damn good; the crowd went wild for them, and they loved the attention.

That same skinny guy from Georgia was first up. He set the bar high; he stayed on for the whole ride. When he dismounted, his crotch stuck out all puffy and swollen like it always does after a ride. His balls had been banging hard into a bull's back. He patted near the area, but women and children were watching, so he didn't touch himself. I knew he couldn't wait to get back to the locker room where he could take them out and hold them. Why was I thinking about that?

Even though I was Second Clown, I couldn't let that fool First Clown put more lives at risk. I worked hard to keep the bull focused on me so the riders could get up defeated and walk away safely. Then I caught sight of Cody.

He was standing in the bleachers near the bullpen, picking at his teeth with a matchbook. He was up after a Canadian guy who was riding Snuff. The bull was named Snuff because he had killed two cowboys already. I felt awful sorry for the Canadian. He had this look like he was headed for the gas chamber. He was young, blonde, and stupid to be riding this sonofabitch.

Snuff tried to climb out of his pen while the Canadian tried to rosin and tie his ropes. He was so scared that he turned bright red, making his blond hair look white.

Then the gate swung open, and Snuff came crashing out, headed straight for the first clown. The Canadian rode real gracefully with the bull bucking like thunder between his legs. The bull crashed into the fence, but the Canuck was able to swing his leg up, and so didn't get hurt. He didn't fall off, either. Then Snuff came straight at me. I had seen worse; I wasn't scared. His horns caught on my overalls, and I hit the ground. I was back up in a jiffy. The horn blast signaled the ride was over. The Canadian untied himself, but the rope was jammed. He frowned and yanked it hard, letting it loose too fast. The bull threw him off hard behind him about ten feet.

Snuff rounded and faced his rider, who was helpless in the dirt. That damn stupid first clown wasn't paying attention, so I pulled rank. As Snuff barreled towards him, I ran between the downed cowboy and the beast, taking it by the horns. He threw me high in the air. I landed on my ass. I was winded, but the cheers from the crowd revived me. The First Clown finally pulled his head out of his ass and lured Snuff down the return gate and out of the arena.

I stood and searched for Cody, hoping he had seen my heroics, but he was already mounted and tied to his steer. I hoped he had seen it, so he would feel stupid for what he said to me by the Coke machine. I never cared what a man thought about me. Something was wrong.

Cody's bull was Prairie Dog. He sat confident when he gave the nod. I knew that bull from the State Rodeo in OKC. He wasn't as easy as he looked. Prairie Dog spins to the left, a problem for right-handers. If Cody was a lefty, he would be okay. But I remember him shaking his fat dick with his right hand. Too bad.

The bull flew out of the pen and spun so fast I thought he would turn into butter. Cody held on good, but then the bucking started. The rope came loose, and Cody smacked real hard into the bull's backside. I thought about those big balls and even bigger dick, and I winced as I watched them slam into the beast's back.

Cody was a man's man. He didn't even act like he was hurting. As I thought about all that flesh between his legs, Blood rushed from my stomach to my crotch. This was the wrong time to get hard. It was seven seconds when Cody came loose and flew off. The horn blared just after he hit the dirt. Prairie dog spun around, put his hoof in the dirt, and snorted.

As an experienced clown, I knew what that meant. I ran straight for Cody, who was still winded from his fall and had his back to the bull as he stood up. Growing up with all those mean-ass cowboys, I learned a few things, including how to tackle someone way bigger than me. It was just a matter of catching him at the right point between his knee and his waist. I headed straight for Cody, and as I grabbed his lower leg to throw him out of harm's way, I was astonished that my hand was also grabbing the head of his cock. It surprised me so much that I forgot to keep my eyes open in the back of my head if you know what I mean. That bull caught my floppy overalls in his horns; I didn't have time to twist out of the way.

I heard this awful ripping sound which wasn't me, just my overalls, thank goodness. I gazed up at Cody, who was smiling. The bull charged again, and Cody just sort of rolled out from under me like I was a piece of paper. The bull came at me, but Darrel The Barrel bumped into him from the side, and he turned away. Cody had a hold of me and was hugging me up next to him to keep the bull from swinging its horns into me. I could feel, even in that brief instant, that his cock was hard. Of course it was; he had just been on the bull. Every cowboy knows they get a big boner right after a bull ride. The first clown waved the bull towards the return gate, and I was out of harm's way. Then I realized the other reason he was holding me up next to him. That bull had ripped off my overalls and tore the flap of my long johns; my ass was showing. He was trying to cover up my bare ass from the crowd. My overalls were across the stadium. The jeans promoter came out with a new pair of overalls for me, and the whole arena busted out laughing. Cody glared down at me and then winked. "Don't put that sweet ass on display, boy. I might want it to myself." Then he let me go, and I put on the overalls. The emptiness was there again, and I thought, "Damn, Brightie, say something. Anything." But I didn't. And Cody walked out of the arena. I had two more bulls to battle.

❦ 4 ❦

SNAKE AND RABBIT

By the time I was done, I ran backstage, and Cody was nowhere in sight. But then I remembered it was only day one, and there was gonna be two more chances to place; I was sure Cody wouldn't miss that. Just then, I heard a noise from the bathroom. Cody was in there rubbing his balls. He motioned me over with a tilt of his head. I didn't hesitate. I just strolled in there and said, "What?"

"That was damn good work out there, kid." He frowned. "What, these?"

He had caught me staring at his swollen balls. I kept quiet.

"They always swell up like that after a ride." Cody glanced over his shoulder. The locker room was empty because it was ladies' barrel racing. Every cowboy watches that. Most don't care who wins; it's all those bouncing titties they come to see. He grabbed my hand and put it on his swollen nut sack.

"They feel hot to you?" He asked me.

I nodded. "Yeah, like over a hundred degrees."

"Go on. Rub 'em," he said gruffly. I thought about it for a second, shrugged, and started rubbing them.

"Aw yeah."

Cody whistled between his teeth. "They took a real beating out there. Just keep doing that nice and slow."

His cock, which had been minding its business over on his side, swelled up. It moved and flopped onto my arm. It grew bigger and lifted towards the ceiling. Now his double coke-can prick was two tall cans of beans stacked together. I couldn't take my eyes off it.

"You like rubbing 'em like that, clown?"

He asked me, but it was more like a statement, so I nodded.

"You a little faggot?"

I didn't know what that was, but I didn't like the sound of it. "No."

"Well, I am." And then he just reached over and grabbed my head, pulling my face up to his, and kissed me like you'd kiss a girl. I was stunned. Up until that very second, I thought he might be fixin' to whup my ass. Now I felt safe. My nerves went all tingly in my belly, and my dick got hard. He forced his tongue deep in my mouth. It was so good.

Cody pushed me into a bathroom stall. We barely fit; he was such a giant. He rubbed me under my overalls with one of those giant hands. His hand felt great down there. He unbuttoned me, and my dick came flying out.

"Boy, that's a damn big cock between your skinny little legs." It came as a whisper. I didn't think he meant it because it was shorter and nowhere near as thick as his.

Cody kissed my neck, my chest, and under my belly button until he reached my cock, which he put in his hand. Then he kissed it! He added his tongue to the kiss. He opened his mouth and swallowed my dick. Never had I felt so good. This must be why all my cowboy buddies wanted a girl. But Cody was no girl, and I sure as hell didn't care. I was glad. All those ladies out there riding circles round the barrels, titties jiggling, made all the cowboys whoop, holler, and throw their hats in the air, I didn't care! I was with a giant cowboy in the men's bathroom, happier than a hog in shit.

Cody kept swallowing, pushing my dick past his tonsils and down his throat. He choked a little, and I said I was sorry, which made him chuckle.

The electricity in my belly was strong now. It was getting warm. All the blood left my head and went down there to fire things up. Suddenly it was like I had to take a piss real bad. I tried to push Cody off my dick, but he was persistent. Something hot came flying out of my dick and straight down Cody's throat. He pulled back, and I watched my dick paint his face white. My knees buckled. I might have fallen if it hadn't been for Cody holding my waist.

I didn't know what I'd just done, but Cody was gonna beat the shit out of me for sure. His face was all slimy. He used his tongue to lick most of it off. We was both out of breath. He used toilet paper to clean the rest. But he wasn't mad. He had a big ole smile.

His hand was on his dick. This whole time he had been rubbing it like a sinner. He stood and put his big paws on my shoulders, forcing me to sit on the toilet. His cock was ready to poke an eye out.

"Now, do you think you can suck mine?"

Sizing up his thick penis, I doubted I could do it. But then I remembered last Thanksgiving. On a dare, I put a whole Turkey drumstick in my mouth, and Mom took a picture. I figured I should at least give it a try.

I put my mouth on the big head, trying to force it in. I sucked hard, which made funny noises. We both laughed. But Cody's face was all sadness. He was about to put his hard dick back in his pants.

"Wait!" I don't know why I shouted it. It was a waste of time. But I closed my eyes and pictured last Thanksgiving. My jaw relaxed, and Cody's fat dick slid right in. I kinda panicked when I thought I couldn't breathe with my mouth full, but I could still get some air through my nose. Then he pushed in further, and I couldn't breathe at all. He bucked like a bull, thrusting deeper each time. As he pulled back for each thrust, I could take a breath. As he went deep, his cock head slid even further down my food hole.

Cody tasted like a salt lick. I gagged a lot and felt like puking, but I concentrated on that salty taste. At last, Cody's bush of hair tickled my nostrils. He didn't go any farther. My throat reminded me of the time I saw a snake swallow a whole rabbit.

I stared up at him. He was making moaning sounds with his eyes closed. He had unsnapped his shirt and was using one hand to play with his nipples while the other one kept my head steady. He was breathing heavy, his chest as big as a clown's barrel, rising and falling in time to his thrusts.

His teats poked out through the thick chest hairs. He became an animal. His breathing grew faster. He said unholy things to me.

"Yeah, suck that cock." Surely he would go to hell. But I liked it. So I might join him there.

"You know you like my big dick in your mouth, Clown Boy." Yes. Yes, I did.

I was hot in my belly, and my dick was hard again. He heaved his big bull cock in and out of my throat at a breakneck pace. My eyes watered; I feared I wouldn't get enough air between strokes. But then the salty flavor of his dick got much saltier, and just then, he pulled it out of my aching mouth.

"Aw, Yeah!" He shouted, and his dick sprayed milky white goo all over me. I clamped my mouth down over his pee-hole to stop the spray but also to swallow it like he swallowed mine. He grabbed me hard by the hair and grunted like a pig. I wanted Cody to pull my hair harder. I wanted him to pull me so hard that I would just be right there with him forever. As more and more of the stuff squirted, my mouth overflowed. I pulled him out, and one more shot landed on my cheek. My mouth was full, so I swallowed. It tasted like salty porridge with buttermilk. I licked the last drops as they fell from his huge pipe.

The announcer's voice came over the loudspeaker announcing the winners of the barrel race. Cowboys and clowns were going to come into this bathroom with warm feelings in their bellies from watching all the jiggling titties. I didn't want them finding out about me and Cody. Apparently, he didn't either because he patted me on the shoulder and gave my hard willy a slap.

"What's your name, kid?" Cody asked as he stuffed his big bloated dick into his underwear.

"Brightie Matthews, sir."

"Brightie, you saved my life and sucked my dick. I owe you a debt of gratitude."

"Yessir." I wasn't sure what he meant.

"Why don't you drop by my motel room tonight? We'll have us a real good time."

I thought that we had a pretty good time already, like nothing could top it. But I was wrong.

THE PURPLE MOUNTAINS

I didn't see Cody at Cracker Barrel for the evening meal. I sat with the First Clown, who talked my ear off about his girl back in N'Awlins. That terrible emptiness crept back. I didn't pay attention to what he was saying. The clown didn't notice; he just kept jabbering to anyone nearby. The food came, and he piped down. I rolled my eyes at Darrel, and he grinned. Afterward, I skipped out on the bonfire, hoping to wash the sweat and dust off.

I got to the Motel just as the sun was setting over the Laramie River Valley, the Medicine Bow Mountains in the distance. It looked a little like Oklahoma, except there were mountains on the horizon. The mountains changed color. That must be what they mean when we sing "Purple Mountain's majesty above the fruited plain."

I bought a Coke out of the machine and figured I'd go to my room to take a bath; then, I remembered it was just a shower. I felt homesick something awful. I was nearly nineteen years old and didn't have no place being homesick, being the hero of the rodeo and all. I saved Cody's life and that Canadian's life too, but there it was just the same. Homesick.

I heard a door open behind me. It was Cody, lighting a cigar in his bathrobe.

"Hey, Brightie."

"Howdy." I couldn't hide my smile.

"You ready to have a good time?"

"Uh, yes, sir."

He put out his cigar on the railing. "Well, come on in. Don't just stand there."

Walking toward the door, my legs turned wobbly. I was excited because I finally knew what that emptiness was. I mostly felt hollow all the time but only noticed it after I saw Cody. He made it go away. Cody grabbed me and pulled me into his room. We got to kissing real fast and hard, like we was wolves fighting over a rabbit.

I got into it this time. When Cody wasn't filling my mouth with his tongue, I pushed my way into his mouth. It tasted like cigar smoke. His bathrobe was tied, but it couldn't stop his huge dick from poking through. It was half hard, rubbing up against my pant leg. I got hard, too; my dick was awful cramped in those jeans.

"Boy, are you sure you ain't a faggot?"

I blushed because all I knew of that word was how the cowboys at school would shout at sissy boys before they kicked 'em in the head. I for sure didn't want to be no faggot.

"N-no, sir."

"No, you ain't a faggot, or no, you ain't sure?"

"I ain't sure."

He picked me up and threw me onto the bed. I laughed because it reminded me of when I was a little kid and my dad would play airplane with me.

"Take your pants off, Brightie."

I wasn't wearing underwear, but I took 'em off all the same. My dick shot up straight like a flagpole.

"Nice. Now your shirt."

"I unsnapped it with one yank, even after Mama told me it wore the shirt out faster. I tossed it onto the floor.

"Shoo-wee, look at you!"

I didn't know what it was, but he liked what he saw.

"Now roll over. I wanna see your ass."

I wasn't used to so much cursing, but I liked it. I rolled over, putting my pecker between my legs so I could lie flat. "Like this?"

"Yep."

He put his hand on my ass and rubbed it back and forth real slow like. I could feel his fingers graze my balls. His hands were warm. I liked how they cut through the chill in the air. He played with my butt cheeks, warming them and spanking them softly. Then he licked his middle finger and rubbed it around my butthole. Up till then, my butthole was something dirty that I had to clean. I never knew it felt so good to have it touched that way. Cody's magic touch had me all jumpy. I was twitching down there.

But then Cody spat on my ass and pressed his finger partway into my hole, then took it back out. It didn't hurt, but it felt weird when he pushed again, going a little deeper. It was like pooping, only back and forth.

Cody knew what he was doing. Pretty soon, he had that finger in all the way to the knuckle. He was prodding and pushing places I never knew existed. My dick started dribbling some clear stuff that looked like cactus juice. Cody caught some of it on his finger and used it to make my hole even more slippery.

Wham! He yanked out his finger and buried his nose in my butt. He kissed my butthole, sticking his tongue in there hard and licking me inside. That was the best move so far. I wriggled and bucked like a bronco, but his mouth never left my ass. He slapped my butt hard.

He lifted his head and leaned forward, whispering in

my ear, "I wish I could fuck your little ass," then returned to my butthole.

I can't say I knew what that would be like, but I didn't care right then because I felt like a cowgirl who just won the barrel race.

He stopped. "Now it's your turn."

I knew what he wanted, but I wasn't sure I should put my mouth there.

"Don't worry, I just showered." His hair was wet, so I knew he wasn't lying.

He took off his bathrobe and squatted on all fours on his bed. His big bull dick dangled between his tree-trunk thighs, resting on the blankets. But my eyes were on his ass.

It was a great big butt, with soft peach fuzz on the cheeks and wiry black hairs down in the crack. The two mounds of his butt were like two honeydew melons side by side. He was such a big man; my whole face could disappear down the valley between them.

He wore shorts outdoors. I could tell because his ass cheeks were white, but his legs were the color of caramel. I leaned in and buried myself in him, slicking up his hairy crack with my tongue. He jumped, and I saw the pucker expand, making a hole where I could fit my tongue inside. I did. As I pressed harder, his hole relaxed, letting in more of my tongue. He shifted his weight, taking both hands and grabbing his butt cheeks. He spread them apart to allow me closer access to his hiney hole. I stuck my tongue in all the way. It tasted like a combination of the time I put a penny in my mouth mixed with the time my mom washed my mouth out with soap for saying "damn." It was a flavor I wouldn't ever order at the ice cream parlor, but now, on my buried tongue, it tasted great.

Again his hole gave way, letting me press my lips up to his ass. It stayed loose.

Now, I've seen horses and dogs do it, so I know

what happens, but I didn't know they could do it in the butt. Bill Gresham says that's not what happens, which is why you never see two boy dogs doing it. But what does he know?

Anyway, right then, when Cody's hole relaxed completely, I knew I needed to put my penis in his butt. I just knew, like second nature. Nobody had to tell me. I dragged my dick across his butt until it lined up, then I put it there, just outside the hole.

Cody urged me on over his shoulder. "Fuck me, Brightie," and that was all I needed.

I told you before that my dick is long but not super thick. I knew it would go in easy. That was why I was surprised when Cody put his hand on my belly to push me back before I was even one-fourth of the way in. He rubbed some Albolene on my dick.

"You ever done this before, Brightie"?

"Nuh-uh."

"Go slow."

I went slow at first. Even with that slippery Albolene, I could only go about halfway before it got too tight. I knew I needed to loosen him up some more. I increased my speed a little, and I felt Cody let me in a little more each time. Once I had enough room, I picked up the pace,

I saw Cody, the big bull-riding cowboy, grab the sheets and grunt with pain. But I couldn't stop. Soon, Cody's grunts changed, and it sounded like he was enjoying it. He relaxed his grip on the sheets and grinned big.

"Damn, Brightie, I thought you was gonna split me in two!"

Now it was my turn to grin.

I still wasn't all the way in. When I leaned in hard, my dick hit a wall. There was still an inch or two to go. I tried to push my way through the wall, but my dick was rock hard and couldn't bend. I thrust a couple of times, banging the wall. Cody yelped.

But then, like everything so far, I just kept doing it, and his cries turned to whispered words like "Sweet Jesus" or "Yeah, right there."

Cody reached back and slapped my ass. I slapped his right back and felt him tighten. Now it was my turn to whisper and moan. It was heaven on Earth.

Cody lifted a leg and rotated on my dick like a corn dog on a stick. I was deep inside him, so I couldn't pop out, even with that slippery lotion all over my dong. I never stopped pumping.

Cody's legs were in the air, so I grabbed his ankles and pushed him to elevate his hole a little. Now I could go deep, hitting that hole with my hips. Except I could see his face, and he was wincing every time I punched that wall. I stopped.

"Am I hurting you"?

"Hell no! Fuck me harder!"

I pounded him as hard as I could. His eyelids fluttered, and instead of wincing, he just moaned like a sheep stuck in a ditch. His big soft dick lay across his thighs, and his giant balls jiggled each time I hit them with my belly.

Cody was happy. He sweated and puffed; a big grin filled the space between his dimples. Staring down at him made me even more excited. Here I was, a lowly rodeo clown, fucking a giant bull rider, his fat cock rolling back and forth on his leg with each thrust of my dick.

I didn't need anything else. That warmth in my belly appeared out of nowhere, turned white hot, and blam! I was filling Cody's hole. It was like a dam burst on a river.

"Damn, that's good!" I shouted, not even caring if I used a curse word. The river drained into the basin, and

I pulled out my dick, causing the milky white sauce to fall out of Cody's crack. He caught it with his big palm and slurped it like it was chicken n' dumplings.

He sat up and kissed me hard, wrapping me in his huge arms. His dick was heavy and stiff.

✿ 6 ✿

RIDING THE BULL

"Okay, now it's your turn," I said to Cody.

He let out a mean laugh. "You couldn't handle it, Brightie. Nobody can."

Now there's one thing I hate, and that's someone telling me I ain't good enough.

"Can too."

"Brightie, it's not that easy. It takes practice. It's painful and dangerous."

"I get stomped and gored by bulls. Hell, it happened twice, just today. I think I can handle it."

I imitated Cody, getting on my haunches. The only difference was that his cock was so heavy it hung downwards like a horse, and my dick stood flat up against my belly. The thought of him going up in me had me excited."

Cody cleared his throat. Just when I thought maybe he was throwing me out, his mustache tickled my butt. He didn't just lick me. He was spitting up my hole. It was weird but good. His fat tongue probed me. If getting fucked was anything like this, it would be easy. But then he took a dry finger and buried it in my hole. It felt painful. But I got used to it.

"It hurts, right?" He was still trying to find a way out

of it. I glanced back and saw his cock standing up, and I knew he wanted me.

"Yeah, but nothing like a bull slamming into me at full speed."

A second dry finger forced its way in. It hurt like hell. I asked him, "Why ain't you using the Albolene?"

Cody spread it all up in my ass. He put in one, two, then three fingers, spreading them and stretching me. It hurt like hell, but I just let out a happy sigh like it was nothing.

"You sure you ain't done this before?"

I saw him stroking his Albolene-covered cock. It had grown fully hard. He had three fingers in me up to the knuckles. I leaned into it and felt even more pain, but like a good cowboy, I didn't say nothing.

"If this is how it feels, I'm ready."

Cody chuckled. "It will be a lot more than three fingers." He pulled his hand out, and my hole snapped shut.

"Let's get going." I wanted to smile like he'd smiled, grunt like he'd grunted.

"Brightie, let's start in a different position. It will feel way better. I'm gonna lie flat, and you can sit on it."

Given the size, I figured it would be like sitting on a barstool. I would never fit him in me; I would just twirl in circles same as I do at the drugstore soda fountain.

But I was determined to do this. I wanted him up inside me like I'd been in him.

He lay flat on the bed, a mountain of muscle with a flesh flagpole. "I'm ready when you are Brightie." His dick glistened with a thick layer of lotion.

I stood over him, spreading my ass cheeks, and lowered myself onto the head. It straddled the hole; it didn't go in. He held me in place with his leg-sized arms and lowered me onto it; this time, my hole landed squarely on the tip. Only a little bit went in before I was stuck.

He told me to push out like I was taking a shit. It made no sense until I did it. Another half-inch went in. There was a forest fire in my ass. I bit my lip, which he saw, and he lifted me right off him. My hole slammed closed.

"Forget it, Brightie." He wore a sad face that just killed me. I couldn't ever see him like that again.

With no warning, I pushed out like I was giving birth to a cow and sat down on his dick, fighting pain and fear, until the head popped inside me. That was the hardest part. Cody's dick was very straight, and it got narrow at the base. I kept pushing, eyes closed. The head crawled its way through my shitter, sliding with ease as the greasy lotion came off.

My ass hurt bad, but it wasn't as bad as being trampled by a bull. I would live. I wanted Cody up inside me so that he would lose that sad face. I opened my eyes, and there was Cody, mouth wide open with surprise.

"No one can do this with me," he confessed, "everyone just gives up."

"I ain't no quitter." Feeling his cock burrow deeper, I smiled.

I wanted him in all the way so I could kiss him. Then I hit the wall. There was still a long way to go. But his dick wasn't as stiff as mine. I leaned to one side, and that huge piece of meat turned the corner and kept going. That was the final obstacle. My asshole was getting a break. I reached the place where his dick narrows, like the handle of a baseball bat. He was smiling up at me, the way a dad smiles when his kid hits a home run. It made the empty feeling leave me. By the time I sat on his hips, the burning pain was gone. I was so full; it was like I had eaten a whole log of liverwurst. I perched in his lap, leaned over, and planted a kiss that could have lasted the whole night. We were joined like a semi to a trailer. Cody was the kingpin, and I was the lock.

Cody was powerful. He was able to pick me up and move me anywhere he wanted. At first, we focused on each other's lips, jumping when this electrical tingle fired up like a light switch each time our mouths came together. But we both wanted more. I was ready for him to hump me.

He placed me face down, my waist on the edge of the bed. I saw one hairy hand to my left, another to my right. He was positioned like a soldier doing push-ups.

"You ready?"

"Fuck me, please, sir."

Cody pulled out most of the way. Each inch brought more pain as his massive cock grew thicker when it got closer to the head. Just when I felt the edge of his dick head, I was about to scream, but he plowed into me again. The relief grew more until he hit the meat wall hard, causing me to cry out in pain."

"Oh god, I'm hurting you." He tried to pull out, but I grabbed one of his giant honeydew melon butt cheeks and pulled him close, guiding his dick around the corner so he could go the whole way.

We kept practicing until he could turn the corner by himself.

"You ready?"

I gave the bull rider's ready nod.

Cody picked up the pace. I wanted to scream at first, but as he moved faster, the pain changed. It wasn't pleasure, at least not by itself. It was strong pressure. When I thought about the man behind me, stretching me and using me like a rubber glove, it turned on a switch. It was like every stroke and every collision was a magnet for something better than pleasure. I think maybe this was ecstasy, like they talk about in the Bible.

If he missed and hit the inner wall, it was painful. But that magnet changed it. That's the only way I could describe it. Like I almost wanted him to miss so I could feel him even more.

Just when I thought it couldn't get better, Cody twisted me like a corkscrew, so I was legs up, on my back. He held my ankles. The pain didn't change. What changed was the magnet. It felt stronger each time our eyes met. Each time Cody smiled at me, his cock filling me up, my antenna picked up even more magnetic pulses. This wasn't the belly tingle that made my dick shoot. It was deeper, like something spiritual. I let him do all the work, which was how he liked it. He put me on my side and joined me in bed. That position let him hold my chest from behind. The angle made him hit the wall before sliding past. I don't know what noises I was making. Cody grunted and growled in my ear, "You like that? You like your big cowboy fucking you with his big cowboy dick?"

I could only moan and nod.

He pulled me so that he was lying on the bed, and I could ride him like a pony. As I did, his cock went so deep inside me I could see where it turned the corner, pressing against my lower belly. He smiled up at me, his two nipples sticking out of his furry chest hair. I touched one, and he jerked. I couldn't tell if he liked it, so I did it again. This time he bucked, forcing his way deeper inside me. I touched both at once, and he went from a pony to a bronco.

We had been fucking for at least three times as long as I had fucked him, and he was still going. My ass was so loose we played a game where he pulled all the way out, even his head, then crashed back in. After ten times, we waited a few seconds, and all the air he forced in me came out in a silent gust. I couldn't fart; I was too loose now. I wondered if this was permanent!

He picked me up and set me down on his hard dick to carry me through the motel room. With each step, we caught each other's eyes. I held his hair between my fingers and kissed his mouth. He said, "Brightie, I want you."

Those words did something to me. My dick dribbled the clear stuff; Cody put the tip of my dick in his mouth and sucked. We returned to the bed. We were deeply connected. On the bed, he could put my whole dick in his mouth. It wasn't long before that hot flood gave its warning. Cody stopped sucking, and it subsided. That made every magnetic pulse turn into that feeling right before you shoot the white stuff. My whole body became a dick about to spray.

I watched Cody; his eyes were closed. He was quivering. I put a hand on his nipple.

"Oh shit, oh fuck. I'm gonna come,"

"Me too."

He pounded into me hard, his chest on top of mine, like the way a mom and dad make babies. I put my arms on his back. He was too muscular; my arms couldn't reach around his body.

Cody's thrusts became ferocious. The battering pain was like coming; then I did. My cock spit hard into Cody's chin. He tilted and caught the next blast in his mouth. He kissed me so that I was tasting his cigar mouth and my own salty juices at the same time.

Cody's jackrabbit pumps came to a sudden stop,

"Oh, holy fuck! Oh damn, Brightie! Oh fuck." There was no mistaking what came next. Stiff as a board, he screwed up his face and made animal noises. Deep inside, past the bend, my belly filled up with streams of hot gravy. Cody had a lot. He lay on top of me, muscles loose now, and let the rest drain into me in little spurts. His sweat smelled like alfalfa and cream. I touched a nipple, and he jerked. He grabbed my hand and put it on his butt. I rubbed his sweaty white ass.

After ten minutes of heavy breathing, we shifted positions. I felt Cody's soft cock come unstuck from the bend. My butt couldn't help it. It thought his big fat dick was a giant poop, so it pushed him out. I heard his cock hit the bed like a steak hitting the cutting board.

Even though he was out now, I still felt the need to empty myself. I realized it was Cody's semen. I wanted to go to the toilet, but Cody had me in an embrace. He noticed me stiffen. I was so loose, I wouldn't be able to stop it.

Cody put a hand out and caught his load as it poured out of me. Watching me with those eyes, he held out his big cupped hand. I had tasted him once before, but not out of my own butt. I tried a sip. It was different. He drank the rest and kissed me, letting a little bit more slip into my mouth. Now it tasted perfect.

We lay side by side, still breathing hard from the rough ride. He flopped his dick across my belly and chest. Even soft, it was a giant.

"Brightie, you are one tough cowboy. I have never gone deep inside a guy until today."

"Me neither."

He chuckled and kissed me. His cheek was like sandpaper as he pulled me close. My asshole was twitching like it needed him up there again. But Cody let go and lay flat. He looked just like the mountains as they rose from the valley floor. Pretty soon, he was snoring. I put my arm over him; when I woke up the next morning, he had done the same.

✸ 7 ✸

STRAIGHT TO HELL

W hile Cody showered, I just lay naked on the mattress, holding my belly. I was sore everywhere. Sore where the bull hit me. Sore throat from swallowing Cody's huge dick. Sore ass because, well, you know. I struggled to my feet and limped into the bathroom to swipe some toothpaste. Cody heard me shuffle in.

"Hey Brightie, c'mere!"

The bathroom was tiny. I had nowhere further to go.

"Where?"

Cody grabbed my arm and pulled me into the shower. "Oh man, did I do that?"

He pointed to a bruise on my flank.

I shook my head. "That was the bull." It came out raspy because my throat hurt. "Your bruises are in places where the sun never shines."

Cody chuckled. He put a soapy finger on my butthole. I jumped, not because it hurt, but because it felt way too good. He soaped my butt, my nuts, and my pecker: the holy trinity.

Each time Cody turned, his huge soft pecker whacked into me.

Despite my pain, I couldn't hold back the warm feeling his big pecker gave me. My dick stood straight out. In a little shower, my hard-on made maneuvering tricky. If Cody's dick were to get hard, we might get trapped! Sure enough, he started to grow.

The only way to keep us from getting tangled was for me to put it in my mouth. I kneeled down and took his swelling dick into my mouth. I knew how big it was gonna grow, so I took advantage of its softness to roll it around, tasting it, putting my tongue in the pee hole. Cody filled the shower stall with his big body. I was cold because no warm water was reaching me. He saw me shiver. He twisted from the hip to allow water to fall on me. The twisting movement forced his hard dick down my throat. I relaxed the muscles, and it moved deeper, blocking my airway. For a moment, I panicked, afraid he might grow too big and I wouldn't be able to move enough to get air. But he had just enough room to pull back and thrust.

I couldn't help myself. I touched myself in an impure manner. Mama says I will go straight to Hell for doing that. I didn't care. I was in heaven right then.

Cody let his head drop back, and more hot water came through. I was soaking wet now. I grabbed his balls with my free hand and played with them. He turned up the hot water, and the tiny bathroom filled with steam. I didn't mind the heat. My skin turned red, but it didn't burn. Through the mist, I could make out his face. He was smiling.

"Damn, boy. For a greenhorn, you sure give good head."

I got flustered because, like I said, I don't like people saying I ain't good enough. It made me more determined to impress him. I pulled back far so only his head was in my mouth, then took a single long glide until he was deep in my craw, and my nose was buried in the hairs above his dick. I kept at it. On the way out, I took advantage of the little bit of extra room in my mouth, swirling my tongue so it licked his whole head before going deep again.

Cody moaned and bucked his hips, banging my head against the shower stall. I could tell he was close because the salty taste was back. He reached over and turned off the hot shower. He extracted his throbbing dick from my mouth.

"Not yet; I still want to fuck you."

I recalled last night and how sore my ass was. I winced remembering it. Lucky for both of us, it was steamy in there, and he didn't see my pained expression. He would've changed his mind. He threw me a towel. I watched his chest muscles ripple as he rubbed himself dry. It kept me hard just watching him.

Back in his bed, he lay flat, greasing his big pole. He grabbed me by the waist and pulled me close. I never let him see my fear. I was all kinds of sore up there. I didn't think I should try it again so soon. But then I thought of those courageous bull riders who might have a sprained ankle or a bum leg, and yet they still got up on the bull. I was determined to do the same with Cody. As I said, his dick was shaped like a Louisville Slugger, wider at the head than down at the base. If I could fit the head in, the rest would be a smooth ride. He was so husky and broad, like a bull. I was scheduled for a re-ride.

I climbed up on top of his dick. With his help, we found the spot where my hole could let his giant head in. I sat down. The burning was something fierce. My face twisted from the pain. I didn't want my cowboy to change his mind, so at the same time, I said, "Mmm, yeah."

I was at the widest part of his head. I couldn't go any further. All of a sudden, Cody thrust upwards, causing the head to pop inside my sore ass. To my surprise, it didn't hurt like I thought. Instead, my ass felt good the same way touching myself in the shower felt good. The walls of my shitter were all tingly. They were like a mosquito bite being scratched. Last night, I was so busy getting used to having anything up there that I hadn't noticed any tingle. The magnetic pulse hadn't started yet, either. This was not pain. It was magic. It was good no matter which direction I moved. I rode him up and down, going deeper with each downstroke. I would straighten my knees until I was almost empty, then plunge down hard. Cody's dick passed that wall at the back and rounded the corner. I was like a hog in shit.

I stared down at Cody, whispering to himself with eyes half closed. I sat down all the way until I was in Cody's lap. He burst into action. He bucked me up and forward until he had my two legs like a wheelbarrow. He pushed me away and then pulled me back close, over and over. My arms held me up in the front, but Cody's hard pounding made me doubt I could hold my weight much longer. There were just too many sensations coming together at the same time. I was moaning in a high pitch like a cowgirl fallen off her horse.

Cody was panting so hard I could feel his breath on my back. He would push me so that only the very tip was inside, then yank me hard, so the whole side of beef stuffed me full. If this was an event at the rodeo, Cody would be given extra points for such long, perfect strokes.

I could tilt my head down and see him going inside me from underneath. My dick was flopping back and forth, Cody's giant bull balls flapping under, hitting mine.

I leaned on one elbow and reached under to touch myself. Cody saw me and decided it was time for a new position.

He caught me by the waist and twirled me towards

him as if I didn't weigh a thing. Now I was facing him with my legs wrapped around his waist. He planted his feet firmly, his hands holding me up by my butt cheeks. I'll wager he could've let go, and I would have stayed right where I was, like a harness hanging off a peg. The tingles turned intense.

Cody curled his neck and took the head of my dick in his mouth. I got a bonus when he bounced me up and down because my dick would slide past his lips. I leaned back until my head and shoulders rested on the mattress. This felt the best because it was angled just right, a straight shot. Cody didn't have to turn any corners to enter or exit my hole. I was so used to him, he could pull his dick out all the way. My ass stayed wide open to welcome him on the return. I was wiggling like a calf being wrestled. Cody picked up the pace. He pushed me back on the bed and got his knees up there to plug me even harder. From that angle, I could play with my dick and watch his go in and out of me. I still couldn't believe that I had that huge thing up in me. My ass was a damn miracle! His breath got short and puffy. He grabbed hold of my dick and stroked it hard. In less than a minute, I was over the edge. My groin burned hot, and a rush of warm, white cream flew out of me and hit the headboard. More kept coming, soaking my nose, my lips, my chest, and finally, my belly.

Cody hauled his giant throbbing pecker out of my ass and jerked it a couple times. He shot all over my face and chest so that both our loads were all over me, running in little rivers down my sides. He hadn't finished. A couple more jerks, and he came again. This time I was ready. I leaned forward and caught the spurt in my mouth. It flew to the back of my throat, choking me. The rest came gushing in, and I swallowed like mashed potatoes at Christmas Dinner. Today it tasted sweeter, like fresh butter before the salt. I sucked on his dick until it was all drained dry. He grinned and told me

I was a real good lay. He said I can have sex with him anytime I want. So that was sex, after all! I didn't know there was sex with two men. What little I heard about it from Bill Gresham, it was only ever a boy and a girl. Now I was confused. I couldn't get pregnant, could I? Worse yet, would I go to hell?

8

A DISTRACTED CLOWN IS A
DEAD CLOWN

I went back to my room to clean up in time for breakfast at Cracker Barrel. While I washed all the sticky stuff off, I wondered how nobody ever explained to me about something so good. I mean, I should be bragging to all the other clowns about how far I shoot and how wide my ass can stretch. The church preacher only said we shouldn't use our hands to play with our willy or we would lose our seeds. Whatever came out of me wasn't no damn seeds. It was wet and slimy. I remembered how we both played with our dicks during the sex, so maybe I sinned. And the preacher says sex outside of marriage is a sin, too, and Cody called it sex. I feared I just wandered dick-first into a wilderness of sin. But Cody was a good man. He had a wedding ring, and that meant a wife and kids, probably. He wouldn't force himself inside me to commit sin. Something that good just couldn't be evil.

I thought about it all through breakfast. Cody wasn't there to answer my questions. The clowns were talking real loud, so the waitress had to come over and tell them all to pipe down.

"Be more respectful like this handsome young man," she said, rubbing my shoulder and back.

The clowns were all envious. You could see it in the

way they watched her hands move. Now envy is a sin, and I don't understand it.

"Why you so quiet, Brightie? Was you out with a girl? They go for handsome, respectful clowns."

Everybody laughed so I didn't have to answer the question. I didn't want to lie, and I didn't want to tell the truth to those clowns. I wasn't sure yet if it was something to talk about. Plus, my throat was all swollen, so being quiet felt better. I struggled to swallow my scrambled eggs.

I limped back to the hotel room. My bruised ribs hurt, and so did my ass. I put on my Little Debbie overalls and my makeup before heading to the arena. I wondered where Cody went all the times he was nowhere to be found. Maybe he just stayed in his room and slept. I wanted to ask him some questions.

At the rodeo, I saw the tall guy from Georgia leaning close and talking to one of the barrel chaser cowgirls. He leaned further, and they kissed. I wished I could kiss Cody like that, out in the open, but something told me that if I did, I would get kicked in the head like the sissies at school. Thinking about it made me mad. I wasn't empty like I was before I got with Cody, but I was confused by it all. Then it dawned on me. I was a faggot. What me and Cody did, that must be what faggots do. Now I was pissed off, but not at any one person. I was mad at the whole world.

I wondered how Cody felt, hanging out with all those mean bull riders, never letting on how bad he wanted to fuck them. I wondered if Bill Gresham would kick my head in if he knew what I'd been doing. He was my best friend. Would he be friends with a faggot?

Mama told me to come back with stories. I was going to have to leave out the most important story so far. I couldn't remember much else. I suppose I could tell her how I saved that Canadian. And no doubt she would be tickled if I told her about when my overalls came flying off, but could I tell her that Cody grabbed me and held my bare ass up to his swelled-up, bull-banged crotch to hide it from the crowd? I could never tell her what happened later on. I had sex outside of marriage with a married man. She wouldn't like that.

Soon it was time for the bull riding. Cody appeared out of nowhere and joined the other riders. He was talking to the long tall cowboy from Georgia, and he pointed right at me. My ears were burning. What could he be saying? The other cowboy grinned and tipped his hat at me. I guess it was something good. I smiled and waved back. The blond-haired Canadian was up first. He was sweating buckets, but at least he wasn't riding Snuff today. The gate flew open, and the bull came out spinning right. The Canadian was a lefty, and he was prepared. He even spurred the bull with long strokes, which didn't go unnoticed by the judges. It was a beautiful ride. The crowd jumped to their feet and roared. He made it past 8 seconds and dismounted on his feet. The judges gave him a 91. The bar was set high. You could see the other cowboys cursing under their breath. Cody gave him a hearty handshake and said something quiet in his ear. The Canadian blushed bright red. I felt the presence of what the preacher called "the green-eyed monster." But there was no time for it.

Another bull came flying out of the pen with rage on his breath. The cowboy fell after two seconds. Even before the bell rang, he charged the fallen rider. This animal had murder on his mind. I was clear across the arena. Luckily the First Clown was on top of it. Before I even got there, the cowboy was up and over the safety rail, and the bull was running down the return gate. I had to stop thinking about Cody. A distracted clown is a dead clown.

Darrel the Barrel asked me if I was okay. I was still limping from last night's fucking. On top of that, I was lightheaded. I said I was fine, and so he left me be.

The Georgian was up next. Now that I saw him with Cody, I listened for his name. It was Kurt Sewell, and he was the first in the average for this rodeo. He was the man to watch. They gave him a bull named White Lightning. That bull was all white with a thunderbolt-shaped patch of black on his hindquarters. Kurt strapped himself down, nodded, and the gate flew open. I tried to get out of the way, but the bull was all over the place. He about near trampled me, but I stepped aside, so he just grazed my left shin. Kurt was the only one who placed yesterday. All he needed was to last 8 seconds to stay in first. He was cautious. No fancy spurring, no grace. He stayed the 8 seconds and won. The rest of the day was about who could push their way into second place. At this point, it was Bruce Dermot, the Canadian, at 91 points.

As Kurt walked off to the locker room, he held his swollen crotch brazenly. He didn't care if the crowds saw him touch himself. He was packing a big gun in his jeans. The chaps he wore just accentuated it even more. I shook my head as if to get a fly out of my hair. I had to keep my mind on clowning. But I watched Kurt until he faded from view. Cody must've seen me because he was staring right back at me when I glanced in his direction. His face didn't give nothing away at first. I thought he was mad, but then a spark flashed in his eyes, and he gave a big grin. I didn't know what it meant.

A few boring rides later, it was Cody's turn. He was bent on scoring high, enough to put Bruce the Canadian in third place. Cody would have to score 91 or more to tie or make 2nd place. He was the last cowboy to ride. The good news for Cody was that he was on a real mean bull, Montana Crush, which meant that if he could stay on, he would score high. The bad news was I had heard bad things about Montana Crush. He was a legend, and he was dangerous. Cody, a giant, looked like a dwarf when he sat up on him.

The gate flew open, and Montana flew out of the pen. He spun so fast he blurred. He bucked so hard that the ground shook. Cody just stayed put, though. and he was spurring back and forth, back and forth, just like when he put his dick in me. Montana didn't like those spurs and threw his hind legs up in the air and kicked out. Cody just kept spurring, and then the bell rang.

The crowd stood up and cheered. It was a small stadium, but it sounded like the roar at the Grand Nationals. Cody flew off the bull and landed flat right at my feet. I bent down to help him up, but he didn't need my help. Then I wanted real bad to hug him. But I just slapped him on the back, and he turned and winked at me. The judges gave him a 91, too, so he was tied with Bruce.

S ince it was the last ride of the day, I followed him into the locker room, where the bull riders were showering. I went to take a piss, and when I came back, it was Cody, Kurt, and Bruce in the showers. I shucked my overalls and stood near Cody since I wanted to be near him, even if I couldn't do anything in front of these other cowboys. My shower barely let any water out, and Cody's was broken, so he was just standing there butt-naked. That's when I noticed that Kurt was getting hard. Even at half mast, it looked enormous because he was so skinny. He had thick, leathery skin hanging down over the head. If he got any harder, I thought he would lose all the blood in his head and pass out. His balls were all red from where they'd slapped into the bull, and they were at least twice the size of Cody's. His dick was longer than mine but not quite as thick. I didn't want to stare too long, so I just turned toward Cody; he was hard too. He was playing with his dick and staring at Bruce the Canadian, who had his back to us. Bruce was bright red again, which made his hair white as snow. I couldn't see but figured he was soaping up his dick.

We were all making eyes at each other, and Bruce

was trying to stay out of it. But when he turned to shut off the water, I saw his hard dick sticking out of his blond bush. Mine was jutting straight out, and not one of us could pretend he wasn't excited. Cody got out of the shower and grabbed his towel to wipe the sweat and grime off his body. Kurt from Georgia toweled off as all our dicks went soft. Not one word was spoken between us until Kurt cleared his throat and said, "329." Cody grinned, and Bruce said nothing, but I could tell he knew what it meant. That was Kurt's room number. I went to my locker, threw my clown clothes in the gym bag, and pulled on my jeans.

I couldn't wait to see what was gonna happen up in 329. I sure hoped Kurt's barrel-chasing girlfriend wasn't staying there with him. When I got to the motel, there was a party going on in Darrel the Barrel's room. A bunch of cowboys were in there whooping and hollering. One of 'em came out and handed me a beer. A couple of the barrel chaser cowgirls were in there, too, laughing and carrying on. It looked like a lot of fun, but not as much fun as what we had planned. I tipped my hat and took the beer with me, saying I'd be back in a while, but I knew none of 'em would be sober enough to notice if I didn't. I gazed up to the third floor, and a light was on in Kurt's room. I clambered up the steps two at a time, and I almost ran right into Bruce. He was at the top of the stairs, coming out of his room. He blushed when he seen me and put his hands in his pockets.

"You going to 329?" I asked.

"Yup."

"C'mon," I said and tried to grab his hand, but he pulled it away, all embarrassed, and just sort of sauntered along behind me real slow. I could tell right then and there that he was even more of a greenhorn than me. What a breakin' in he was about to get!

When I approached the room, I could hear Kurt

and Cody inside. I peeked through the curtain and saw them rassling on the bed. Bruce knocked on the door real formal like, and Kurt jumped up, straightening his clothes, and answered the door. Bruce tried to back up, but I was standing right behind him, so he stepped on my boots.

Kurt cleared his throat and said, "Come on in, don't be shy."

I sorta pushed Bruce off my boots, and he had to go into the room. Then I shut the door, and Kurt put his arm over Bruce's neck and tried to kiss him. I went over to Cody on the bed and jumped up beside him. We kissed like lovers. Bruce tried to wriggle out of Kurt's headlock. Kurt stopped what he was doing.

"What's wrong, cowboy?"

"I ain't no faggot," Bruce stammered.

There was that awful word again. I hate that word. So did Kurt, apparently.

"Well, I ain't no faggot neither. I just like to get nekkid with my buddies for a little fun. I bet you do too."

"I guess, eh?" Bruce admitted.

Kurt started taking off his clothes. Me and Cody had stopped kissing to watch the show, and we were enjoying it an awful lot. Kurt undid his pearl snaps one at a time, then loosened his belt buckle.

He stopped there for a minute and stared at Bruce, "C'mon cowboy, ain't you gonna help me off with these duds?"

Bruce blushed, but he undid the top button on Kurt's jeans. Kurt was skinny, and the jeans practically slid off him and bunched up at his ankles. He had on briefs, and they was sticking straight out. Bruce went down on his knees to lower Kurt's underpants, and Kurt's dick leaped out of there, slapping against Bruce's jaw. That was real exciting. I told you Kurt had a long one, and when it was hard, it stretched out even further. It weren't anything as fat as mine, but it was longer by far. His dick had outgrown the skin, which was tucked up tightly under the head.

I leaned over on Cody next to me. He was showing through his jeans. That baseball bat dick of his was pretty near halfway to his knee. I could see it throbbing, pushing against his pants leg. I reached over and rubbed my hand on it. Bruce didn't have a clue what to do at this point, so Kurt stood him up and undressed him.

We could hear whoops and hollers coming from Darrel's party downstairs. It was real nice being up there, away from all the ladies. I hadn't gotten more than a quick glance at Bruce's dick in the shower, and I was curious. Cody noticed 'cause I stopped rubbing him so hard down there. He chuckled and whacked me real gentle on the side of my head. Bruce wasn't wearing underwear, and so it wasn't long till my curiosity was satisfied. He had light blond pubic hairs, almost like you could see right through 'em. Kurt bent down and took Bruce's soft pink dick into his mouth. Bruce turned all red and made little noises. At first, he wanted to push Kurt away, but then he threw himself into it, humping his mouth. Bruce's dick turned bigger 'cause I could see it in Kurt's throat, making a little bump there every time it went down. Kurt picked Bruce up and threw him down on the bed beside me and Cody, then went back to sucking him. I undid Cody's top button and pulled on his zipper. His dick was so hard I couldn't pull it out of his pant leg. He winked at me and tugged on his jeans, sliding them over his big ass and kicking them off his ankles. Then he opened up my jeans, pushed me on my back, and sucked my dick. Cody's dick was plenty long, but I couldn't reach it in that position.

Bruce was lying right next to him, and he could. He didn't need no instruction at this point; he just leaned right over and licked the end of Cody's dick. He struggled to put it in his mouth. Since I was left with nothing to suck on, I twisted around until I could suck on Kurt's. It tasted saltier than Cody's. It was thin enough that I had no problem breathing while it was in my mouth. I gagged when he'd pump it down my throat, but I didn't get sore like with Cody. When I put Cody's cock in my mouth last night, it took a lot of work to slide it all the way down 'cause it would stick right about where my tonsils were. Cody had to scrape past all that, and it hurt. But Kurt's was thin enough that it went down like I was the sword swallower at the circus.

Cody played with my ass, and I got excited. Kurt's ass wasn't very big, and I wanted to play with Cody's, so I lifted my head and reached for him. That gave Kurt the idea that I was going for the switch, and so he let go of Bruce's dick and reached for mine. Bruce let Cody drop, and he switched to sucking on Kurt. Cody didn't miss Bruce too much because the boy still hadn't figured out how to get that big dick past his teeth and inside his mouth. Cody let go of my dick so Kurt could suck on me. I didn't want to see Cody's dick going to waste, so I opened wide and put it in my mouth. I knew how to handle his meat; pretty soon he was pounding on my tonsils. I caught Bruce staring in amazement as I let inch after inch of Cody slide into my mouth. I tried to fit it past my tonsils like I did with Kurt, but tonight it wouldn't go; my throat was too sore. I couldn't see Cody's face, but I hoped he wasn't disappointed. Now Bruce didn't have anyone sucking on him. He didn't mind since he was going to town on Kurt's dick. He stroked the Georgian's massive balls. They were like two Florida oranges, swollen as they were. Bruce looked about ready to pop and needed to cool off a bit.

Cody pulled his dick out of my mouth and sat on his haunches, his big ass in my face. I put my tongue up his butt. Because of the broken shower, he hadn't washed down there. It smelled strong of sweat, bull, and rodeo dust. That got me more excited. I had to pull away from Kurt to get a good angle on Cody to work my tongue up there. Kurt got back with Bruce, and it sounded like they were kissing. I buried my nose in Cody's big sweaty buttcheeks. I couldn't see much of anything except them hairs in the crack and the end of his dick swinging down. I had to rely on my sense of smell. When I came up for air, I saw Kurt wasn't kissing Bruce on the mouth; he was kissing his ass like I was doing to Cody.

That moment was all Cody needed; he caught me off guard, tackling me, slamming me on my back, and lifting me up to him so he could lick my ass. I was still stretched and sore, but man, his tongue felt nice. My legs were hooked over his shoulders, and he was licking my balls when he wasn't down my crack. I had another good shot at Kurt's dangling dick, so I reached out my tongue like a bullfrog and caught the end of it. Kurt kept his tongue buried in Bruce's rear end, but he moved over and squatted down on my face, so I could take his whole dick down my throat again. He came up off Bruce's ass, and soon I could see his finger sliding in and out of that boy's blond butthole.

Kurt had a technique where he would turn his dick, so I could feel it rubbing on the sides of my throat. It made me gag some, but it felt too good to stop. Then I heard Bruce say the first thing in a long time,

"Mmm. Yeah. Fuck me, man." I didn't think Bruce could handle what came next. Kurt pulled his dick out of my mouth and plopped it next to Bruce's butthole.

"Are you sure you can take it?" he asked.

"Fuck me. Just fuck me." The Canadian who 'weren't no faggot' was singing a different tune.

Kurt found some petroleum jelly and rubbed it on his dick and all up in Bruce's pink hole. He tried to shove it in all in one go, but Bruce yelped and told him to wait. Kurt stayed in part way, but he didn't go no farther. Bruce looked like he'd just been stomped on by a bull. There was tears in the corners of his eyes, but he was a bull-rider, and he musta learned not to be afraid of pain like I'd done as a clown. He bucked up, and when he came down, Kurt's dick slid in real far. I had a good view of it from where I was. It musta hurt real bad. But Bruce just turned red and made a mean face. "Fuck me, come on, harder."

I liked the sound of that. I turned to Cody, who was staring at me from over my dick and balls while he licked my ass. I was ready, and I didn't even have to say anything. Before I knew it, Cody was ready. I was as slippery as greased lightning. I guess my ass was a fast learner 'cause the burning when he put his head in wasn't as bad as even this morning. I was used to him and could relax, so it didn't hurt much at all, even though it was the size of two stacked vegetable cans and just as hard. When he fit the fat part past my ass-crack, it slid into the thinner part near the base. He turned that sharp corner like he was driving a Corvette in there.

I glanced over at Bruce. He wasn't as red now, but he was huffing a lot. I thought about what it must be like to have a real long skinny one up there and how it must not hurt as bad as Cody. I wanted to try it. But now was not the time, 'cause I had a big fat log of a cock up my ass, and there wasn't no room for anything else.

Cody leaned forward and got into a push-up position. His arms were as big as another man's legs. I got hot just watching his muscles flex on the upstroke. His knees would come down to the bed, and then when he lifted up, bang, his muscles would grow. It felt like his dick was growing at the same time, but it was just because he was pulling out, and the fat part was stretching me open more.

I checked on Kurt and Bruce, and I got a nice surprise. Kurt saw me, and he picked up Bruce and moved him so his balls were hanging down into my face. When he pumped into Bruce, his dick and balls would graze my lips. I reached up and took Bruce's soft pink dick into my mouth. I stayed hard when Cody's dick was up my ass, but Bruce was soft. I sucked on his dick until he was hard. It smelled like Snickers bars, and it tasted almost as sweet. It fit in my mouth without stretching or gagging me. It was easy.

Then I got another surprise. Cody lifted me off his dick so I was a little closer to him, and then he put my dick in his mouth. We must have made a pretty picture: Kurt was plowing Bruce on all fours, whose dick I was sucking while Cody fucked me and sucked me at the same time. Because I had to lift my hindquarters a bit so Cody could put more of my dick in his mouth, he couldn't go inside me all the way. The fat part of his dick was stretching me hard, and it hurt something awful. Then everything switched.

Now Kurt was licking Cody's asshole, and Bruce was sucking on my dick. Kurt put his dick up Cody's butt. Cody went down on Bruce. It was like when we played musical chairs in grade school. And I was left without a chair. Then Kurt motioned me over. Cody was sitting in Kurt's lap. My big bull rider wanted me to fuck him at the same time as Kurt. I was astonished. I didn't think you could do that, but Kurt said you can. Cody must have wanted to know how it felt to get fucked by a dick as big as his own. Kurt pulled Cody to his chest. He let his dick most of the way out of Cody's ass and pushed my dick up next to his. Mine wouldn't go in because it was fatter than Kurt's. He pulled all the way out, and I got mine wedged into the opening. Kurt held his skin from the other side so it wrapped around my dick partway and turned into one thick, long, strange dick. When I plowed in all the way, Kurt's popped in beside mine. I had never imagined anything so good. Every time we moved, our dicks slid over each other. Cody was pounding on the sheets and cussing, saying stuff like "Jesus H. Christ. Fuck, yeah!"

Did he praise the Lord with that mouth? Kurt put his tongue in my ear and licked it. That was real nice. We locked lips. Kurt's kisses tasted like unsweet iced tea. We were so into the kiss we didn't pay attention; our dicks popped out of Cody's ass. He just reached back and put them back in. He was stretchy enough now that they went right in. I wondered how he had such a big, loose hole, and I found out later, but that's another story I'll tell later. Bruce was the odd man out. Cody wasn't giving him much attention because he kept shouting all those curse words and didn't have time to suck him. Bruce was pretty smart, though. He perched over the three of us, spreading open Cody's legs and positioning his ass over his dick. Cody reached down with one hand and put his dick up to Bruce's crack. I don't think Bruce knew what he was getting himself into, but like I said, he was a bull rider, and pain was no stranger to him. Cody pushed his enormous cock in there, and Bruce pushed back. Here I thought I was brave. Bruce was a champion. But then I remembered he had a warm-up already, and I don't think this was his first time. Cody entered him with a loud pop. Bruce slid halfway down Cody's giant pole, squatting like a frog. He was crying from the pain, but it didn't stop him from continuing to slide up and down. Bull riders are tough. I reached out and rubbed Bruce's pink penis until it swelled up and dribbled.

The rubbing and sliding was all just a little too good for me. I was close. Kurt was too. He huffed and licked his lips, sweat pouring down his forehead into his eyes. His thin dick, pressed against mine inside Cody, pulsed real hard. His throbbing was kinda contagious. All of a sudden, he pushed in deep, said, "I'm gonna come," and shot his load. I could feel his much longer cock move way past my dick and fill Cody. The juice was hot. My dick was slippery with Kurt's cum. I leaned my head back and moaned, and I came, too. There wasn't any room for it since Cody was already so full. It back-washed toward my crotch and sprayed out the edges of the bull rider's stretched hole. When we pulled out, some cream came with us and made a puddle on the bed below Cody's ass. I guess that hose-down put Cody over the edge because no sooner had we pulled out than he exploded halfway inside Bruce. He pulled out, shot all over Bruce's back, and splattered it in his clean white hair. He flipped Bruce over onto his back and finished him off, sucking his dick hard again until he came in big white blobs all over his mustache and down his chin; Kurt was still hard. I was too. Kurt flipped me over onto my back, putting his hard, skinny, long dick up my hole. It went right in, no problem. It tickled. Kurt laughed. "It's like throwing a hotdog down a hallway."

Cody stood behind Kurt and tried to push his dick up his ass, but it was no use. Kurt was too skinny; there was no way. So Bruce moved back there and put his blond beauty in Kurt's ass. Cody sat his ass down next to me so I could lick the cream out. From that position, Kurt could lean forward while he was fucking me and suck on Cody's dick. I was amazed we were going at it again like this. I guess having four people makes you four times as excited. I played with my dick while Kurt fucked me. His dick was skinny but hard as wrought iron; it wouldn't go around the corner. It was a bolt of lightning every time he hit up against my walls. It shouldn't feel so good, but it did. And I loved his skin sliding against me up there, all loose. When Cody fucked me, there wasn't any room for me to do anything fancy. But with Kurt, I could tighten down real hard and then let go, so he slid in all of a sudden and rammed up to that lightning wall.

Bruce knew how to fuck. Kurt kept moaning and then lowing like a cow. I had my tongue up Cody's ass. There was still some stuff up there that needed cleaning. I sucked and tongued him until it came out slow, like the last bit of jelly sliding out of the jar.

I twisted my ass to get into a corkscrew with Kurt. His balls hung low and slapped up against my ass every time he plowed in. I rubbed my hands over Cody's big white asscheeks. Sometimes I could feel when Bruce was going deep into Kurt 'cause Kurt's dick would tighten up and push on a place inside me that felt real nice and made my dick leak. Kurt was fast, and he came up inside me after just a couple of minutes.

Bruce took over. His dick was thicker than Kurt's but nowhere near as long. His balls were tight, like Cody's. His head was a lot bigger than the rest of him. When it went in, I could almost hear it make a pop. He had a pretty good technique like a good bull rider should. When he pulled back, he made sure to tease my asscrack by making me think he was on the way out, and then blam! He would fill it right back up again. I squeezed on the Canadian's thick dick with my ass muscles, and his eyes widened. I don't think Kurt had done that to him. I don't think the girls he'd been with could, either.

I grinned, proud. He leaned forward and pounded into me. Sweat dripped off him onto my chest. He put Cody's dickhead in his mouth and licked it, but so far, I was the only one who could suck more than the tip. Cody reached out and pinched Bruce's teats, which took him by surprise. He twisted them real hard, and they stood up bright pink against his milky white skin. He went red. Air came out of his mouth in blasts. He pulled out so far that I thought he was gonna pop out for sure, but then he plowed right back in all the way, hitting that lightning place hard and then shooting. I could feel his hot juice filling my ass. Then he stood up and walked over to the bathroom, where Kurt was taking a shower. He climbed in with him.

I was alone with Cody. He picked me up like a rag doll and sat me down on his cock. That night, I had been with much smaller cocks. My ass burned as his huge dick went up inside me. I must say, though, that there wasn't any feeling quite like it when he turned the corner, and I was stuffed full, sitting in my bull rider's lap. It was like we belonged this way. He kissed me hard on the lips and bucked his dick up into me. I would fly up and come down hard on his lap, traveling up and down the length of his Louisville Slugger. When I landed hard, I saw his dick poking out of my stomach. I loved seeing stuff like that. It set me into fits like a bucking bronco. I rode up, down, and sideways too. I must have looked like a paddle ball; I was flying up and down so fast. He was sliding in and out real easy 'cause both Kurt and Bruce had left their stuff up inside me, and it was coating the walls of my ass.

Cody closed his eyes and moaned. I sat down all the way. I wanted him to come inside me, not on me. I mustered up all the strength I had and clamped real hard on his dick. That sent him over. He leaned back, bucked up hard, and shot his load. It felt like a hose up my ass. Gobs of hot milk came from his monster cock and filled my shitter to the limit. When he took his dick out, I shot a load of cream out my ass. It landed on his belly and made a splat. He loved that. I watched as he squeezed the last drops of come out of his dick. I didn't need anything. I was so hot from all the fucking. All I had to do was aim my dick at Cody, tug it a few times, and it shot out and splattered all over him. Cody licked some of it from his fingers. I took a towel and wiped him down.

Bruce and Kurt seemed to be having a good time in

the shower, so we put our clothes on and headed back to his room for a wash-up. Some of the drunk rodeo cowboys were out on the balcony, and they squinted at us as we walked by. I wondered what they would think if they knew what they'd just missed out on. I didn't think I'd ever find out. Boy, was I wrong.

❧ 10 ❧

MORNING WOOD

T he next day, I got my chance to find out what drunk rodeo cowboys think of what we did. And I discovered how Cody could take all that dick in his ass with hardly a blink. But I'm getting ahead of myself.

This was Sunday, the finals. I woke up early, spooning next to Cody. He had a morning boner that jutted between my legs. He was still snoring. I brought the rock-hard monster close to my ass. I needed to scoot my ass away from the cowboy to get the end of his hard monster positioned properly. Cody's arm was draped over me, so it took some fancy maneuvers.

At last, his cock head touched my butthole. I felt like a cat in heat. I needed it all inside me. To my surprise, it took little effort to pop the head in. I snuggled my way back to Cody, allowing the entire length of his giant dick to fill my insides. When his short and curlies tickled my bottom, he slipped around the corner up inside me, and I pushed myself tight against his sleeping body. I nodded off to sleep.

A few minutes later, I awoke to the oddest sensation. My innards were warm. Cody was awake. He gave a lopsided grin. I swelled fuller and fuller.

"What are you doing"?

"I can't fuck in the morning until I empty my bladder."

"But you were hard!"

"That's a piss boner. Besides, I want you real clean."

I was mad, but then I had to admit, as the last few sprays of piss filled my gut, it was arousing. I had a boner.

Cody picked me up, cock still deep inside me, and carried me to the toilet.

"Can you hold it when I pull out"?

I nodded, unsure but wanting to please Cody.

"Okay, hold it in until I say!"

He lifted me off of him and set me on the toilet. I clamped tight. My tummy was cramping, and I needed to let go. Cody gave the sign, and I let loose a flood of his piss and my poop. It was smooth, not like when I had the stomach flu. When it was all out, it was out.

"You all clean, Brightie?"

"Yep," I said, letting the last dribbles trickle into the toilet.

"Can you take me?"

In answer, I planted my lips on his. We kissed like we was trying to eat each other's tonsils.

Cody knew how hard it could be to take his big dick, "Now Brightie, you sure you're ready to take me again? It's gonna hurt, I promise you."

"Getting gored by a bull hurts, and I take it just fine." I was defiant, even though I liked how Cody was acting like a concerned father with his son.

"Don't say I didn't warn you."

He knelt and held his mouth to my butthole. He dug his tongue into me. He was licking my insides like they were a bowl of cake mix. It felt so good, I shivered.

Cody pulled his tongue out to ask, "Am I hurting you, Brightie?"

I didn't need to answer. I pushed his head hard so his tongue was right against my hole. He licked my insides again. I held on to the towel rack so's I wouldn't fall over.

Cody must've loved licking my ass. Twenty minutes later, he was still rubbing his whiskers up against my hole. He found places in me I never knew existed. I felt my whole body spasm as clear stuff leaked from my hard penis.

"Cody, I can't wait anymore. Put it in me."

Obediently, he removed his tongue. My slippery hole snapped closed, but not for long. With expert style, Cody stood up and slipped his cock inside my sore ass. I was so relaxed from the licking I didn't feel the pain until he was all the way in, plugging away at me like an oil derrick. It burned like hell.

I had to groan, or I would have cried. With Cody's cock deep inside me, I wanted to wail. Every square inch of my insides was raw, like someone had taken a belt sander to my poop chute. Yet I wanted Cody filling me up more than I wanted to end the pain.

Cody knew he was doing something awful up in me. He might have seen my eyes full of tears, or he may have heard a groan. He grabbed the tub of Albolene and a small metal tin off the nightstand. Cody took a fistful of Albolene and pulled out. He plastered my butthole with it and wiped off the rest by stroking his dick. From the tin, he handed me a little glass vial wrapped in canvas.

"Pinch this until it snaps, and sniff hard."

It smelled like model glue and dirty feet. I fell forward onto the bed. Somewhere on Mars, Cody rammed back inside me. My heart throbbed in my ears. I was too dizzy for pain.

After a minute, I came back down. Cody's cock was plunging in and out of me like an oil derrick. The burning pain was gone. I was loose and slippery, and I liked it. Cody slapped my ass hard.

"You can't get enough of me, can you?" He grunted after each word.

I knew what he wanted to hear, "No, sir."

"You love it when I put my big cock in your tight little hole."

"I love your big cock inside me, sir."

"All the way inside?"

"All the way"

Cody licked his lips. "Good! You're the only one who can take it all. I'm never gonna stop fucking you."

The pain was coming back in waves. I trembled. Cody reached for another vial and popped it open. He held it to my nose. I ain't too sure what happened next because I was somewhere else. When I came back down in my body, I was flat on my back, legs in the air, my guts stretching and shrinking in a slow, steady trot. Cody was coming in for the final lap. His rhythm changed. Two fast swings of the hips, one slow. I was in pain, but I wanted to make Cody happy. I put on a brave face.

"You want my cum inside you?"

I nodded.

"You want me to shoot my load way up inside you?"

"Yes," I held back a groan until it came out a sigh.

"Tell me you want it."

I grunted and whispered, "Sir, I need you to fill me with your load." I kept grunting to mask the hurt deep in my gut. It drove Cody wild.

His rhythm switched to a gallop. In-out-in-out fast as lightning, he stampeded through my shitter. I remembered just then how to make it happen fast. I reached up and pinched his teats between my fingers. Cody's eyes locked with mine. Now he was the one grunting. The harder I squeezed, the faster he fucked me.

"Oh shit, Brightie. Oh fuck. I'm gonna come." He

threw back his head and drove his giant pole into places it had never gone before.

He pinched one of my nipples hard. A fire lit up inside my balls.

"Yes!" Cody yelled so loud they heard him in Idaho. "Yes, oh Brightie, oh fuck I'm gonna, I'm gonna," and then he did.

I don't know how to explain this next part. While Cody was shooting cum inside me, he was squeezing ever harder on my teat. That fire in my balls erupted. I shuddered, and a hot glob of my own cum landed on my forehead. My hands were on Cody's nipples. Three more giant bursts of semen covered my left eye, my mouth, and the headboard. Cody had closed his eyes, but now they were wide with amazement.

"Brightie, did you just come?"

I bit my bottom lip and nodded.

Cody beamed. "I fucked you so hard, you orgasmed. Look, Ma, no hands!" I was grinning with pride when he bent down to kiss me. We laughed into each other's mouths. After a couple of minutes, the kissing slowed down. Cody's monster came loose. It snaked its way out of my bowel and out my butthole. Then came a milk bucket of Cody's semen. He caught all of it with his giant cupped hand and fed it to me. Like an obedient child, I drank the milky white soup and licked the bowl clean.

❧ II ❧

A SINGLE MAN

We lay on his bed. I felt sad because this was the last day. I wanted Cody to win so we could celebrate. I stared at his wedding ring. My eyes welled up.

"Hey, hey. What's this about?" Cody put his giant thumb on my cheek and wiped away the tears.

"Nothing." That answer just never seems to work. Cody held my chin and gazed at me.

"Come on, Brightie. You can talk to me."

I shrugged. I put my hand on his. I liked how it felt to have that strong hand on my chin. I couldn't look away. I reached for his finger and tapped his wedding ring.

Cody frowned. He didn't get it. I tapped twice, hard, on his wedding ring.

"My ring?" He laughed. "That ain't real."

"You ain't got no wife?"

Cody picked me up like a bag of lemons and plopped me down on top of him. He chuckled. "No way, Brightie. I would kill a woman with this thing." His dick throbbed against my hip.

"Then why in heck are you wearing it?"

"It's complicated. It might take a while to explain."

"We got time. I'm listening."

"So, you remember that first night? How you fucked me?"

I nodded.

"I let a lot of cowboys fuck me. See, I already explained how I can't have normal relations with a woman on account of my size. But a man needs sex. I had never met a cowboy who could take my cock all the way inside him. You are the first."

"I ain't a cowboy; I'm a clown."

"You are the best fucking thing to happen to me, but let me finish my story. So I can't fuck anyone, man or woman. That is, I can't fuck, not unless I'm the one getting fucked. Lucky for me, I am surrounded by horny cowboys who would stick their dicks inside a gumball machine if it got them off."

I glanced at his crotch. Even soft, that thing is way too big for any human to take. I must be Superman.

"The thing with cowboys...you can ask them to keep quiet, but they talk—a lot. Word travels fast. Cody likes it up the butt. This is both good and bad."

"How so?"

"It's good because I get cowboys lining up for sex out my motel room door. I love good cowboy dick, and I had more than I knew what to do with. I had nights where ten cowboys had their way with me one after the other."

I felt a flush of anger that might be jealousy. I wanted Cody to myself.

"The bad part is that we're riding steer in the Bible Belt. Not everyone was excited by the rumors. I had to fool the religious folk. They're dangerous. But they fool easily. Any of them come sidling up to me with a nasty sneer and questions, I just point to my wedding ring and say, 'My wife would be awfully displeased to hear you say that.' It works great."

I knew my face gave me away. I was hot behind the

ears thinking of all those men putting it in Cody like he was a whore. Cody held me close.

"Brightie, I know that's a lot to hear. But hear this: I never met anyone like you before. You're a miracle."

I couldn't hold it in. "Sounds like you met a lot of men like me. Way too many. I can't share you with the whole rodeo."

And before I could let him see me cry, I threw on my jeans and ran out of there.

❦ 12 ❧
SONNY

Breakfast was hell on Earth. Cowboys were just like Cody said. Whispering and pointing, they musta thought I was a zoo animal. Someone I never seen before sits next to me and starts asking questions that would make a whore blush.

"Hey Brightie, I heard you was the first one that could take Cody. Is that true?"

I just ate my cornflakes, so he went on. "Not only that, you had room for Kurt and Cody at the same time."

"You heard that?"

The guy stammered. "Hey, sorry, I'm Sonny Weiser. I ride bareback broncs. Do you want to go somewhere a little more private to have this conversation?"

"I don't want to have this conversation at all."

I stood up and limped out of the dining room. I heard cackles and hoots. They figured I was limping from the sex with Cody. Worst of all, they were right. My innards were one big bruise.

Behind me, I hear the clop-clopping of cowboy boots hurrying to catch up to me. It was Sonny.

"Hey, don't mind them. I'll bet half of them wish they could do what you did. And the other half wish they could have you like Cody did."

"Which half are you?"

He giggled nervously. "I guess the second half."

Sonny was a handsome man. He had a trim mustache. He wore faded jeans that showed off a mysterious bulge hemmed in by his leather chaps. I stared, wondering what was going on down there. He wore a white cowboy hat. I guess I figured he was a good guy because I let him continue.

"See, nobody knows much about me. I'm a private guy."

"Come on, what's this about?"

Sonny blushed. We were at the motel. He took me by my arm. It wasn't rude; it was polite. "I would like to discuss this in private, and my room is right here."

I figured we had an hour until we all had to be at the arena. I shrugged.

Inside the room, Sonny spilled the beans. He put his hand to his crotch.

"I saw you staring, and I'm happy to explain."

Sonny's crotch was huge. It was unnatural. Sonny continued.

"Riding bareback is brutal to your private parts. I love riding, but the pain was too much. My dick wasn't real big, but my balls were. A few years back, they turned purple. I went to a doctor who told me I had damaged a vein. He drained me, and it felt a lot better. He said if I kept riding, I would lose my balls and maybe my life. I would have to quit. I live to ride, Brightie. It would be like dying either way. But then I heard about this doctor in Juárez who did...procedures."

"What kind of procedures?"

"He injects liquid silicone into your balls to make them bigger."

"But you said your balls were too big already."

"With all that rubber, there's a cushioning effect. I was willing to try it if it meant I could ride without pain.

63

"So I went to see him for a procedure. He filled my sac with silicone. When I saw what the hypodermic did to my balls right before my eyes, I got hard. I'm like a normal six inches, but the doctor said he could make me bigger down there too. I went for it. In five minutes, I was a lot bigger. I couldn't believe how good it was to have a thicker penis. It was so good that I went back a few times. Too many times."

"Did it work? Did your balls stop hurting?"

"No pain. It was a miracle. I kept going. Each time, my ride got easier. But -- well, see for yourself."

He dropped his chaps and jeans to reveal a huge deformed cock and grapefruit balls.

"Man! That is unreal!"

Sonny hung his head. "Yeah, it is."

"I get why you came to me." If Cody was two cans of beans, Sonny was a coffee can. I couldn't help myself. I lifted the man's penis. It weighed four or five pounds. The shaft was soft and bumpy. The head was hiding down a tunnel of flesh. His balls were heavier than his dick. They covered his thighs.

It was such a powerful package; I just had to do something.

I kneeled and put my whole face in the gigantic foreskin-like opening that led to his penis. I heard Sonny moan when my tongue reached his head. As I licked it, Sonny's dick grew a little. His head came forward and popped out of its hiding place. It was so small, surrounded by all the thickened skin. When he was totally hard, his penis was unreal, like a cartoon. I stood back to consider the doctor's handiwork.

"I'll understand if you don't want to go through with it." His face hardened, and his head dropped a couple notches.

I'm a rodeo clown. I don't let cowboys be trampled, not by a bull, not by anything. That frown on his face activated some protective instinct in me. He was thicker than anyone I'd ever seen. He wasn't likely to get what he asked for, but it was worth a try.

Sonny was well prepared. He had Albolene and a tin of those glass tubes. I smeared him up and put a gob in my butthole. I leaned forward onto the bed and held my butt cheeks apart. He hefted his log with the head at my hole. He needed two hands to keep it held in place. I popped the glass and inhaled deeply.

The next minute was a blur. I came to and didn't feel him. Sonny was on the bed beside me, hanging his head in disgrace.

"You can't do it either. It's useless."

That was a challenge. I pushed him back on the bed and straddled him like a horse. His dick was way shorter than Cody's, so it was easy to maneuver. Sonny had gone soft, but he got excited when he saw I was going all the way with him. His head reappeared rock-hard. I took as much of him in me as I could, which wasn't much, then I blew out all my air and whiffed that stuff three times in a row. Before I went somewhere far away, I used gravity to sit on his dong until it had nowhere to go but up inside me.

I must have sat right because when I came back from outer space, Sonny had a huge smile. He bucked up inside me. My weight held him down so's his cock stayed buried inside me. He would have popped out if I had let him slide it back and forth.

It was painful. I pretended to enjoy it, but hiding behind that smile was an ugly face of agony. Sonny wasn't like Cody, who had so much length to work with. It was only like someone had a short bit of their arm inside me from the elbow to the bicep, nothing more.

Sonny would have needed another inch to hit the wall. He was all the way in and hadn't hit it once. My bruised and battered belly was relieved he had a short one. My butthole had given up fighting the invasion. I ignored the little rips and spasms that told me I was getting hurt. I concentrated on how great it was having Sonny inside me. It was the fattest dick I had ever seen. I loved how it made me so full. Not the kind of full I got when Cody filled me deep, but it was stretching my ass and filling my butt like a giant flesh balloon. The weight felt like a sandbag was holding me down. Those thoughts clouded over as more flashes of blinding pain tore through me.

Sonny's sweet smile made all of it worth it. He didn't give much warning. He moaned and rolled his eyes back, then years of semen filled the back of my shitter. When most men would have stopped, more kept coming out the edges of my ass while Sonny was still in me. He bucked and thrashed. As much pain as I was in, to see Sonny shoot me full of his sperm took it all away.

"Oh fuck, Brightie. Oh fuck you're good!" I winced at his foul language. It didn't sound right coming from a handsome cowboy.

I rolled off of him, leaving a puddle of his semen on his pubic area. I couldn't hold it back. More body fluids came pouring out my butthole. It made a big wet blob on the bed.

"I'll clean it. Go get ready for the rodeo. Thank you." Sonny kissed my forehead.

As I limped towards the arena, my worn-out asshole still gaping under my overalls, I thought about the difference between Cody and Sonny. Not their dicks, but the way they made love. Cody never kissed my forehead. I would have slugged him if he did. He was everything I could ever want for a companion. When I ran out on him, did I destroy my chance for a better life? I can be a stubborn ass. I felt lightheaded walking into the arena. I drank a Coca-Cola to revive me.

THE FINALS

This time, I watched the bronco riders with interest. I watched the way they kept smacking hard into the horse. I thought about Sonny's new balls, protected from injury by a medical miracle. I thought about how sad he must be to never have sex no more. I had to be his first in a long time. When it was Sonny's turn, I saw him mount bareback and land on a cushion of rubbery dick and balls. He kept his spurs in motion, never touched himself, the horse, or the rigging, and rode to an easy score of 91. He dismounted airborne, landing on his feet. Only I knew what caused his jeans to shake so hard upon landing.

Every once in a while, I caught a cowboy leering at me. I pretended not to notice, but they could see my ears turn red. Some of them had faces not even a mother could love. Most of them just looked like men back home, the kind you might sit next to in church or at the movies. None of them were like Cody. I scanned the stadium but didn't see him. I just saw more rodeo folks glaring at me in a disrespectful manner. Even the dumb-ass First Clown was making eyes at me like you make at a girl. Cody did this. I was no longer a man to these cowboys. Cody had stolen my respect and manhood.

It was time for bull riding. Bruce was up first. He needed 74 points to take the lead. Kurt only needed to stay on for the ride. He could score just 60 points and still walk away a winner. Cody needed the same points as Bruce going into the round, but I didn't give a shit. I hoped Bruce would win.

Bruce rode a bull called Boston Brahmin. I didn't know that bull, but he looked pretty sinister. I was ready to interfere if anything happened to the blonde Canadian boy. But Bruce didn't need my help or anyone else's. He rode masterfully, soaring skyward, spurring, arm outstretched. The bull was so furious I could see steam coming out his nose. But the madder he got, the more points he scored for Bruce. Bruce dismounted after the bell with a huge grin. He never turned his back on the bull. Boston found the safety gate and trotted himself out of the arena. Bruce scored 90. The crowd roared. He was in the lead with 183 points, but Curt had 160 and another ride. The only other cowboy who could knock Bruce off the throne was Cody. Where was he?

I scanned the arena, ignoring every lecherous lip-licker until I saw him by himself in the bleachers. His face was stone. He stared out into space through dark sunglasses. It hurt to look at him, so I turned away. I saw him glance in my direction out of the corner of my eye. I pretended not to notice.

Cody was paired with a bull called Mud Beast. I clowned against Mud Beast a few times. He's a shitty bull. He's dangerous and lazy. He'll take any shortcut to throw a man off his back, scoring low, then stomp his ribs out of spite. I felt sorry for Cody, even if I was pissed off. No cowboy should have to deal with such a sorry excuse for a bull.

Cody swung his leg up and over the bull. From my angle, the sun was behind him, so he was just a shadow. I got sad and empty when I saw the outline of his leg, with his huge cock making its way toward his knee. I thought about all the beatings he must take on a bull, same as Bruce, but he didn't need medical help. He was just a rugged cowboy. How many of his fellow riders had left their cum in his ass? How many leered at him the way they were leering at me? Today, all eyes were on me. I was cheap clown meat to Cody's prime rib.

Was that the difference? Was it because I was a clown that they stared at me so ugly and shameless? Cody rode bulls. I just distracted them. It was like I was beneath everyone on the rodeo ladder.

I was thinking too long because I only snapped out of it right when Mud Beast lumbered out of the chute with Cody, bucking once or twice, then using his hind legs to buck up and toss Cody over his horns. I froze for a heartbeat; then, I got busy. Cody was caught in the horns. He held on by the armpits. The bull stood still and tried to bite him. The eight seconds blasted.

The First Clown was stumped. None of us had ever seen a situation so bad. I grabbed Darrel and rolled the barrel right up to Mud Beast, but the bull didn't care. He just kept tearing at Cody's shirt. I didn't know what I was doing, but Cody nodded and motioned us closer. He planted his boots on the barrel and used it to do a backflip right back onto the bull. The whole arena leaped to their feet and cheered. Cody slid off Mud Beast, and I sent the bull out the Safety Gate.

Bruce won in points, but Cody won popularity for sure. Everyone wanted his autograph. Before he turned to his fans, he focused on me and lifted an eyebrow.

"Brightie, I can't thank you enough."

My eyes were stinging when he turned and walked away. I watched his perfect, round butt in those tight jeans and realized how stupid I had been. Of course, he let other cowboys fuck him. Look at the way his ass moves when he walks. It would be a waste not to fuck that beautiful butt.

❦ 14 ❦

PASS AROUND CLOWN

I wanted to run after him, but Darrel grabbed me.

"Brightie, that was brilliant! Come on! We got two hours before the bus leaves. The steer wrestlers bought beer; let's go!"

The party was in Darrel's room, the same as last night. The cowboys gave me the same lustful stares, and now I understood what they meant. The beer was good, and pretty soon, I was crocked. I got tired and lay flat on my face on the bed. I felt someone's hands on my shoulders. Darrel must be trying to hustle my drunk clown ass on the bus.

"Just a minute, man, I'm almost ready."

It wasn't Darrel. I don't know who it was. He was holding me down. His friend was pulling my pants down. I couldn't escape. I wriggled and shouted, but one of them put a sock in my mouth and pushed me into the pillow. I could barely breathe.

Then it started. I heard someone spit and wipe it on my ass. And then they were inside me. I don't know who he was, but he was rough. He may have been small, but he was still rough enough to hurt.

He shouted, "This clown is looser than a bucket of night crawlers!" There was laughter all around me.

Part of me wanted this. I wanted to be like Cody.

But he took those cowboys lying on his back, not face down in a pillow. This wasn't the same.

I was scared. I didn't have any say in what happened. I was a clown for cowboys to use. The first one grunted twice and left his mess in me. Another cowboy stepped in. This one was a lot bigger and just as rough. I gave in. It shames me to say that I liked it. It felt good being paid so much attention. There were hands on my legs and shoulders. I could feel naked dicks graze me, waiting to jump in and fuck the dirty hole left behind by the guy before. I wanted more; it was humiliating.

"Look at that! He's hard. He likes it. That boy's got a pussy where his ass belongs!"

I lost count. Most of these cowboys had little dicks with hair triggers. They shot their load in under a minute. I remember one guy whose huge legs pressed against mine. His dick was thick and one of the few that rounded the bend. He was the best one. But none of them were anywhere near as good as Cody.

One cowboy was like a pencil with an eraser on the end. I thought he was going to poke a hole in me. Where was Darrel? Was he lined up to fuck me too?

Getting fucked by so many men at once makes you dizzy, like drinking a few beers. I passed out for a while.

When I woke up, there was a fistfight. Nobody was holding me down, so I rolled over to see what was going on. Darrel and Cody were kicking the shit out of the few cowboys still in the room. The others had either left or were chased out. Cody saw I was up, so he wasted no time knocking out the First Clown, who had huge legs and a big, thick dick. He was worth remembering. When the guys that were left saw the clown take a fall, they ran out, Darrel chasing them down the stairs.

"Cody." My breath was weak and shaky.

❧ 15 ❧
UNRAPING

He wrapped my naked body in a bedsheet and picked me up. I thought of that statue of Jesus at the Pope's mansion. Without a word, he carried me up to his room. He brought a washcloth and a basin of hot water. He wiped my backside.

"Cody, I didn't mean what I said."

"I know." He continued to clean me gently.

Darrel poked his head into the room. "Y'all need anything? The bus is leaving in five minutes."

I tried to get out of Cody's manly grip, but he held on.

"Cody, I gotta be on that bus."

"I have a truck. I'm taking you home."

Home. Mama wanted stories. What could I ever tell her? I stood, shaky as a newborn colt.

"Let me take a shower."

The water wasn't hot enough to take off the shame. I caught a glimpse of myself in the mirror. I had a black eye, and it was all puffy. When did that happen? Did my cowboy rapists punch me? I guess so. I'd tell Mama it was a bull that caught me off guard.

Cody smiled when I came back to him. I sat in his lap and kissed him on the lips. He didn't kiss back.

Then tears came. I couldn't undo what I said. I

couldn't unrape myself. Cody didn't want me anymore. I was a used clown.

"Hey, hey, what's all this?"

He took that same massive thumb and wiped tears off my cheeks.

"You don't want me anymore."

Cody was shocked. "You went through a lot just now."

"So you don't want me."

He said, "I don't want to hurt you; there's a difference."

I bristled. "I see how you look at me, like I'm disgusting."

Cody shook me. "What's disgusting is what those assholes did to my baby."

Did he just call me his baby?

"Cody, I need you to make love to me."

He wouldn't meet my eyes. "How could you want that after what they did?"

I wiped my nose. "The whole time, I compared them to you. I wanted you. I wanted it to be you." And before I could cry, I held his head close to mine and kissed him. He tried to pull away, but he couldn't hide what was growing in his lap. I licked behind his ear and rubbed his nipples. I whispered.

"If you don't fuck me now, it will never be erased. I need you to put it all back where it belongs."

Cody stood up. I figured I'd messed up again. But Cody closed the door and drew the curtains. He left a table lamp on but turned off the rest.

"Believe it or not, I know what you mean." He smiled, rubbing his long, thick cock that was trapped in a pant leg now. "Are you sure this is what you want?"

I nodded.

He peeled his jeans off, freeing his monster. He gave me a vial of amyl nitrite. "You're gonna need this more than ever."

I half-smiled. What he didn't know about Sonny wouldn't hurt him. Like that cowboy said, I was loose as a bucket of worms.

He applied Albolene and put one, two, three fingers in me. They went in easily. He frowned. He added his pinky. Still no resistance. Then his thumb. I sighed. It was great to be with Cody again. Soon he had his whole hand wedged in my hole. It felt too big to fit, but with a bit of pressure, he pushed the entire fist in there up to the wrist.

"Am I hurting you?"

I shook my head.

Cody removed his greasy fist. He stroked his cock until it was slick with the Albolene.

"Do you want me to..." I straddled him before he could finish his sentence, putting my tongue deep in his mouth.

I pinched the vial and inhaled the vapors. Quickly, before the fumes took me out of the room, I held Cody's huge cockhead to my ass and slipped it in. I felt the room spin more and more, but I knew I was sliding down the length of his fat pole. I remember him hitting the wall, then turning the corner before I landed on the narrow part at the base.

I don't remember Cody picking me up and putting me on the bathroom counter, but that's where I came to. He smiled again and winked. And much too gently, he ground his hips against my ass and pulled back. He inched his way forward, touching hips to butt. I needed him to be the animal in bed I remembered from before tonight.

"Hard, Cody. Deep and hard. Make me feel it."

"But-" I put a finger to his lips before kissing them.

"If you don't, then they win."

A light came on in his eyes. Now he understood.

"You ready?"

"You bet"

"I'm gonna fuck you silly."

I leaned back against the bathroom mirror and closed my eyes. Cody carried me back to the bed, his dick inside me like a hot dog on a stick.

He began fucking me hard, fast, and long. He went deep, so much deeper than those tiny dicks in Darrel's room. With each thrust, I erased a little penis from my memory. There goes the first guy. There goes his little friend. There goes the fucking first clown and his pencil dick. Round and round in circles, I let go of the cowboy rape dick by dick, thrust by thrust, until only Cody was there, where he belonged. I put my hand on my belly so I could rub where Cody was pounding my insides. He smiled.

"You like that, Brightie?"

"Mmmmm."

"Am I better than those losers tonight?"

"So much better."

"Are you going to let me fuck you again?"

"Anywhere, any time."

Forehead sweat dripped on my chest. I tasted it. It made me hard. I realized I hadn't been hard since I passed out in the middle of the rape. Cody was like medicine.

My hard dick rose to slap Cody's belly. He patted it lovingly.

"Let me do a magic trick," Cody said. "This always works on me; let's see if it works on you."

He pulled way, way out until the very thickest part of his cock was almost out.

He pointed to my dick. "Now watch."

He rubbed the thick part of his cock along the first few inches of my shitter. There was strong pressure. Then the magic trick happened.

"Whoa!" my dick released a long clear stream of sticky fluid. "What is that"?

"That's pre-cum. I'm squeezing the magic spot. Most men don't know it exists."

"Most men must live empty lives," I said.

"Here's the best part." Cody ran his finger through the clear puddle and held it to my lips. It tasted sweet and metallic. Greedy Cody wiped up the rest for himself as he plunged in. I gasped in sudden pain, the good kind of pain. Cody didn't seem worried. That was what I was afraid I had lost. Cody could fuck me good and hurt me, but he didn't worry. He was so worried before.

I didn't want this to end, but Cody's big nipples were impossible to resist. I leaned upwards and clasped onto one like a young calf. His whole body shook. His breath sped up. So did mine. I kept sucking. It felt like I was sucking electricity because both our bodies began to crackle like lightning. When he touched my nipple, I exploded everywhere. It flew in my nose, my hair, on Cody's chest hair.

Cody didn't notice. He threw his head back like he was about to sneeze.

"Oh fuck! Brightie, you fucking sexy clown!"

And a warm shower of Cody's spunk filled my insides, marking me as his property with sweat and semen. We stayed together, holding each other, until it was checkout time.

"We better call your folks and let them know you're alright."

✖ 16 ✖

REST AREA

Cody stroked my hair in the truck while we rolled down the Interstate.

"Brightie, I forgot to tell you the good news. It's excellent news, in fact."

"Hm?" I was drifting off to sleep.

"You ever been to Brazil?"

That woke me up. "Brazil? Is that in Mexico?"

Cody laughed at my geography skills.

"It's in South America, you pinhead!"

"Okay, so what about it?"

"Well, see, they got the rodeo down there. Just like ours."

"I didn't know." I thought cowboys was just an American thing.

"The president of the Brazilian Rodeo Association was in Laramie this weekend. He saw you and me with that bull."

I sat up straight.

"He wants to fly both of us down there for the biggest rodeo of the year. We'd have to go as a team. You would be First Clown when I ride."

"Are you shitting me?" I had to remember to stop cursing like that before I saw Mama again.

"Nope. It's in some little town called Barretos. We would have a lot of traveling to do."

I gave Cody's old pickup truck the once over.

"Would this thing make it?"

Cody laughed again.

"They're gonna fly us down there! Honestly, what are they teaching kids these days?"

"I graduated two years ago, so I got no idea."

Cody ignored that smart-ass answer. "We'd be stars down there."

"Yes."

"Yes, what?" He took his eyes off the road and smiled.

"Yes, I'll go to Brazil with you. Yes, I'll be your First Clown."

After Denver, the road back to Oklahoma was long and boring. We were in Colorado heading into Kansas when I fell asleep. I woke up when we stopped somewhere. My head was in Cody's lap. I smiled up at him.

"Why'd we stop?"

"Rest Area. You need to piss?"

We were alone. There was nothing but cornfields in every direction. In the toilet, the lights were out. It was spooky, but I felt no fear walking in there with Cody. The moon was the only light, enough to show us where to aim.

Cody took a long time to start and a long time to finish pissing. I was done, and he was still going strong. I saw the moonlight bouncing off the firehose between his legs. It made me hard.

"Something come up?" I could hear Cody's smile in the dark.

I'd bet he could hear me blush.

"We're almost home." Cody put a hand on my belly. "Did you want–"

I cut him off with a kiss. We were both hard. Our

79

dicks pressed against our bellies when we hugged our bodies tight. Cody was so tall, and his cock was so long it was almost up to my chin. I put him in my mouth and let him slide to the back of my throat. I sat on the toilet so Cody could use my mouth. I took him deep. He grunted like a pig as he moved past my tonsils and down my food hole. It was so good to have him inside me. It didn't matter what hole. I wanted to be stuffed full. And I was.

Cody put his hands on my ears and rubbed them real soft-like; shivers went up my spine.

"Oh Brightie, you do it so good." He pressed deep. I couldn't get any air. I put my hands on his muscular ass and pulled him in. I waited until I saw stars and pushed his hips hard so that he unblocked my airway. I coughed up some spit. I took two deep breaths and pulled him to me again. My throat burned. I saw stars again. This time when I pushed, he pulled out all the way.

All in one move, he pulled me to my feet, spun me, and put his dick against my butthole.

"You want this, Brightie?"

I nodded quickly. He pushed into me hard. My ass had bruises on its bruises, but it still could take Cody. It was like I was built just to handle him. He filled me up, turned the corner, and filled me up some more. I heard the big man crying.

"What is it?"

"I'm sorry, Brightie, I just never in my whole life found someone who could go all the way with me. I'm so afraid of losing you."

"I ain't leaving, so shut up and fuck me." My mama would have washed my mouth out with soap.

Cody hugged me from behind, lifting my feet off the ground while he jackhammered in and out of me. In the dark, with just the sounds of the Kansas cornfield, our moans sounded like a tornado. Over and over, he filled me and emptied me out. He chewed on my ear and played with my teats. This angle, where he was lifting me up off the ground, put a lot of extra pressure on that magic spot. Pretty soon, I was leaking. I wiped some and held it out to Cody, who ate it like a horse eats sugar cubes. There was so much of it, enough for both of us.

The sex just got better each time. The more we knew about each other, the more ways we could make stuff feel good. Cody knew every inch of my guts. He knew where to press, where to twist, where to push, and where to pound. Each time he made me moan or whimper, it turned him on more. I wanted to return the favors, but the way he held me, I couldn't do much. Then I realized he liked it that way. He wanted to be the one giving it all. And when I relaxed and let him, it was the best feeling in the world. I didn't have to do anything but relax, let Cody hold me up, and let him pound my hole until he found release. I rested my head on his shoulder. He was able to kiss me, filling my mouth with his big tongue. We were connected.

We both wanted it to last forever. But we were still far from home, and Cody had started to slow down, which meant one thing; he was close.

Cody nibbled my ear. The soft breaths turned into panting. I reached down and grabbed my dick, but Cody pulled my hand away and rubbed me himself. He wanted to be in charge of everything. His big hand was so rough against my dick. It was good, too good. I jerked like a bucking bronco. He was going too fast. I wanted to come when he did. But when my breath quickened, so did his.

"Are you gonna—"

"I'm gonna—"

And the pitch-black restroom filled with white moonlight as we both shot our loads. Mine sprayed all over the toilet stall. Cody's landed deep inside me where it belonged. He eased my feet to the floor. He released his bear hug. I tried to stand, but my legs gave way. It was only the strength of Cody's dick that kept me from falling to the floor. He hugged me to him, and we waited. His dick was still rock hard. I thought he would turn soft, but he didn't. If anything, he stretched me open even more than before.

His voice tickled my ear, "You got another one in you?"

I smiled.

He rocked his hips slowly but then faster until it became urgent, like when you gotta pee real bad. He held my waist so he could fuck even faster. It was different this time, but it was good. Cody was focused on himself. My hands were free. I found one of his nipples and twisted it hard. It made him go faster. It was so much rougher than before, but it still felt so good. I grabbed my dick and rubbed it. I knew it was a sin, but I didn't care. I needed it.

Cody hollered, taking me by surprise, and squirted up inside me. I was still pulling on my dick. Cody lifted me high in the air so that his dick and all his semen fell out of my ass. I heard it splat on the bathroom floor.

Next was a big surprise. Cody took my hand off my dick. I thought he was gonna rub me himself, but I was wrong. It was hard to see in the dark toilet stall, but I recognized those big round mounds of ass in the moonlight. He bent forward, putting my dick on his butthole. He spat on his hand and rubbed my shaft until it was slick. Cody bellowed like a cow giving birth. His ass gave way, and I plowed my way in. I forgot how sweet it felt. Cody pounded the wall of the stall and stomped his foot. I was hurting him. I tried to pull away, but he shoved me in further. His breath slowed down, and pretty soon, he was moaning. That was my signal to get moving. I pushed past his back wall until my balls brushed his butt cheeks.

"Fuck me, Brightie!"

I didn't need any further instructions. I had been

pretty close when Cody turned the tables. Between the tingling in my asshole and the excitement of being in his, it didn't take me long. I slid back and forth past that back wall a few dozen times, and then my belly turned hot.

"Do it, man! Give it to me." Cody begged.

His ass caught the moonlight. I saw my thick dick stretching him, moving in and out between the mounds of butt muscles. It was so sexy; I couldn't hold it. A bunch of cum flowed out of me into the man I loved. His chute became slippery with my semen. It kept coming in buckets. When I finally grew soft and let it out, Cody released a small river of white spunk onto the floor. I caught what I could in my hand, and Cody lapped it up like an obedient terrier.

The sun was coming up as we stumbled our way back to the truck.

NAP AND A BATH

At home, Mama insisted Cody stay for supper.

"You boys must be awful tired. Why don't you go up to Brightie's room and take a nap."

My bed was too small for two, but we thought we could make it work. We needed our sleep, and being so close made it impossible. I took the floor.

When we woke up, Cody and I both needed a bath. I told him to go first. I stripped to my boxers and asked him about Brazil while he lathered up and soaked in the tub. I saw old scars and recent bruises where the bulls had left their mark. With Mom so close by, I didn't know if I should try anything. I touched each scar and asked for the story. Some of them were just the usual, falling from the bull and getting stomped. One scar on his neck surprised me. Before he was into bull riding, he did steer wrestling. That sorta explains why his body is so strong. Even though they grind down the horns to make them rounded instead of spiked, one steer was just so ornery he threw his head with full force into Cody's neck. It hit an artery. Cody still doesn't know what happened next; he just woke up in the hospital with everyone telling him he was lucky to be alive.

The whole time he talked, I had my hand on that scar. He covered my hand with his. Then it was only natural to lean in and kiss him. The bathroom door was closed. My younger brothers were in school, so we had the place to ourselves.

The kissing turned serious. Cody's big cock rose out of the water like a submarine periscope. All of a sudden, Cody pulled me into the bath. It made a crash and a splash. I held my finger to my lips.

"Brightie, you okay up there?"

"I'm fine, Mom!"

"What happened?" I was grateful that she was still hollering from the kitchen and didn't climb the stairs to investigate.

"Nothing. Don't worry."

Cody was kissing my neck and biting my ear while I was fibbing to my mom. It was exciting. I was as hard as Cody. We were sitting face to face in the tub. Cody took my cock and held it against his. I knew from gym class that I was big...maybe even the biggest in my graduating class. But Cody was huge. Pressed up against his giant meat, I couldn't scarcely believe how much thicker and longer he was. He moved his hand up and down in a steady rhythm. Pressed together, we were too big for Cody's one hand by itself. I put mine on the other side and followed his moves. We rubbed ourselves good. I sensed the blood throbbing in Cody's dick.

He growled. It was a new sound; I wasn't sure what it meant. The growls repeated every thirty seconds. Then it was every twenty seconds. A tingling built in my belly while Cody's growls became fast pig grunts. He kept quiet for my mother's sake as best he could. I kept my breath soft. Cody pushed his dick hard against mine so he was aimed at my mouth. Three quick grunts, and he let loose a milk pail's worth of white cum that landed all over my face. I couldn't see nothing, so Cody's mouth took my dick by surprise. He lifted my ass and went all the way down. It was too much; I blew my load down his pie hole.

❧ 18 ❧

SUPPER

S upper was my favorite: Chicken in Dressing.
Mom served Cody first.

"What was that ruckus I heard upstairs?" She
asked me as she plopped a generous helping of chicken
on my plate.

"We were rassling over who got to go first."

"And who won"?

"I did, ma'am." Cody smiled, and it put Mama at
ease.

"Brightie, Do you see this man? You are never going
to win at rassling him. Besides, guests always go first."

"We was just play fighting, nothing serious."

Mom asked questions like I was on trial for murder.
Thank God Cody knew how to play this game too.

"Did you meet a lot of other nice cowboys like
Cody"?

I had to pick through the memories and offer up
some characters. "Sure, there was Darrel the Barrel, uh,
Bruce from Canada, Kurt from Georgia." I almost let
slip Sonny, but he needed to stay secret.

"That's nice. Are they all so well-behaved like Mr.
Cameron here?"

Cody interrupted. "It's Cody, ma'am. Mr. Cameron's
my father."

Mom giggled.

"How come you missed the bus, Brightie?" She was at it again.

"It, well..." I was stumped. Cody jumped in.

"Clinton is right on the way to McKinney. Your boy saved my life yesterday; it was the least I could do to drive him home."

"I expected you here so much earlier." Jeez, she wasn't gonna stop.

Cody was in charge of this fib. "Ma'am, we were both so tired, we thought it best to stop at a rest area and get some sleep. It was the middle of the night, or we would have called. Sorry to worry you like that, ma'am."

"That's alright, Cody. I'm just glad you brought my son home safe and in one piece."

I thought about how he about split me in two that first night, and a chuckle escaped before I could hold it back.

Mom could have asked for an explanation, but let it be. I couldn't explain my way around that laugh.

After strawberry rhubarb pie, during a cup of Chock Full O' Nuts coffee, Cody dropped the bomb.

"Mrs. Matthews, your son and I got noticed at the rodeo."

She leaned forward.

"See, there was this talent scout from Brazil. They got rodeo real big down there. Just like ours – well, almost."

Mom nodded and pursed her lips but said nothing.

"Anyways, he wants to fly us both down to Brazil for an exhibition there. All expenses paid."

Mom was conflicted. She wanted me to see the world and always told me so, but by "world," she meant Kansas City, not Brazil.

"They got communist troubles in Brazil, don't they?"

"I haven't heard." Cody was surprised by the cross-examination.

She continued, "They say if something doesn't change, they'll be just like Cuba by 1965."

"Who's they, Mom?"

"I read it in the Christian Science Monitor."

I had to admit, that's a pretty good source of news, all things considered. I played my Ace. "It sounds like I better go now before it's too late to see it."

I let that hang in the air like burnt toast.

"You said they're paying all expenses?"

Cody nodded.

"You promise to take good care of Brightie? Don't let nothing bad happen to him?"

"Yes, ma'am. I'll make sure Brightie is safe and well taken care of."

Hearing those words made me warm inside. I knew he could 'take care' of me better (and deeper) than any cowboy.

"How much is Brightie gonna need to go there? We ain't exactly made of money."

"No, ma'am. This is paid and paid well. We get two hundred dollars a piece, not counting meals and motel.

Mom almost blew coffee out her nose. Even I was shocked.

Mom relaxed. "Go, Brightie! Go to Brazil. You found your calling. Remember your mama when you're rich and famous in Hollywood."

❧ 19 ❧

OKC BUS TOILET

Our first flight was from Dallas Love Airport, so I took a bus to Texas. Cody talked me into coming early so we could spend time at his house in McKinney before the big journey. By "spend time," he meant get nekkid and fuck. I could scarcely wait.

The bus from Clinton was almost empty. It was a six-hour trip with a change of bus in OKC. That first leg to Oklahoma City was quick, but I had to pee the whole way, and it was the old kind without the toilet. When we stopped, I checked, and there were 45 minutes until the bus to Dallas. The men's room in OKC was a den of sin. Not a man in there needed to use the facilities except me. When I walked in, it was like a chicken flying into a fox den.

Cowboys, dads, and businessmen with briefcases rubbed their crotches while they watched me piss. Some licked their lips, and others played with their belt buckles. No sooner was I done peeing, still shaking it out, when a cowboy with a crooked hat grabbed my wrists from behind and dragged me into a stall. It happened so fast; I didn't have time to fight back. Then crooked-hat undid his jeans and pulled out a real nice dick. It wasn't a big one, but it just looked right. Everything was in proportion. His balls swung chin height. Pretty soon, they were smacking me hard. It was nice to suck a dick without having to come up for air. He filled my mouth but didn't reach my tonsils. I pushed on his flat butt until he touched the back of my throat. He sucked in his breath; I bet his wife never did nothing like that for him.

A businessman in a trench coat appeared from under the next stall. He was quick. He undid my zipper and pulled my dick out, stroking it to get it hard. I could tell by his stare that he liked the big ones like mine. He knew how to handle it. His nose was in my pubic hairs. It felt good. I almost missed it when the crooked cowboy came in my mouth. He zipped up and backed out of the stall. I was on my back, moaning. That trench coat could sure suck some dick! He knew when to stop to make it last. He was a greedy sonofabitch. Wanted me all to himself.

A middle-aged dad forced his way into the stall, waiting for me to unzip him. He grabbed my head and rubbed it in his crotch. It smelled like children. The poor guy was desperate for sex.

I unzipped him. A fat, heavy wiener popped out. He wasn't as fat as Cody and only half as long. Still, it was hard work. He had enough to push past my tonsils. My throat was awful sore, and I wanted to tell him to go away. But then I glimpsed his face. He was in heaven. At last, he had found someone to take him deep. He thought I was gonna reject him. His smile changed. He was heartbroken. I couldn't do that to him. I pulled down his jeans enough to get a good grip on his butt cheeks. I rammed him in as deep as he could go. When I looked up, the smile was twice as wide as before.

My hungry businessman knew just when to stop and when to start up again. In between, he slapped his cheek with my big cock, licking the clear sticky stuff like it was ice cream.

The fat-dicked Dad seemed like he could go forever. His wife was lucky, even if she stunk at dicksucking. I know women want a man who takes forever because that's what Bill Gresham told me. I ain't no woman, and I wanted Dad to get on with it. I found his nipples through his undershirt and tweaked 'em hard. His legs buckled, and I had to hold him up by his butt with one hand while I pinched him hard with the other. It worked like magic. He shot, and I swallowed a bunch of sperm that woulda been children were it not for me. He was gone quicker than he came.

I saw disappointment as I closed the stall door behind him. Half a dozen men were waiting to use my throat. I figured the businessman would take care of them...slowly.

I tapped him on the shoulder, and he nodded. In twenty seconds, I came hard down his throat. He made gobbling noises like he was eating mashed potatoes and gravy.

I saw his watch and groaned because I had lost track of time. It was a minute past the departure time. I zipped up and ran out of there.

🌿 20 🌿

BUS TO DALLAS

When I banged on the door, the driver had already fired up and was backing out of the stall. I would hate to tell Cody why I missed the bus. Lucky for me, the driver pulled forward and parked. He opened the door.

"Come on then."

"Oh, thank you! Thank you! I'm so sorry."

He shook his head and backed out, heading non-stop for Dallas. This bus was packed in the front, but a dozen rows of empty seats were at the back in the smoking area. I sat in the last row. The bathroom was right there, which was fine by me at first.

I realized right away why no one was sitting back there. That toilet stunk. Combined with the cigarette fumes, it made me want to throw up.

I grabbed my suitcase and moved eight rows up. The smell was still there, but only like how you smell a cigar from far away.

There was a red-haired cowboy in the seat opposite me. When I noticed him, he tipped his hat. When he was done, he put his tipping hand in his lap. I thought maybe he had jock itch because he was scratching along his left thigh. I knew it was rude to stare, but it became hard to turn away once I saw what he was scratching at.

He watched me watching him. I put my hand on my right thigh and rubbed my dick. With a flick of his head, he motioned me over to him. He gave me the aisle seat.

"Name's Brightie." I offered my hand. The cowboy said nothing. I let my hand drop. I guess sinners don't make small talk. In the time it takes to blow your nose, that cowboy had his big freckled dick out and was waiting for me to do the same. There weren't no one behind us, and the nearest person in front was four rows up. I was on the aisle, so I was hesitant.

"Come on, man!" He sounded mean. But he was awful easy on the eyes. I shrugged and pulled out my dick. When we were both hard, I took a sec to compare. I was bigger, but not by much. He didn't care. He put his hand on my dick and waited for me to do the same. I was tired out, and I would have gone back to my seat if this cowboy hadn't had a firm grip on my dick. I grabbed hold of his freckled rod and gave it a few tugs. In under a minute, the cowboy had painted the back of the seat in front of him. He let go of me and put it away. I was relieved. I wanted to save something for Cody!

When we was both zipped up, he turned to look out the window. He still didn't have a name to give me. I think a lot of men like it that way. Hell, I like it that way - but it's awkward. I moved one seat back so I wouldn't see him ignoring me.

At 3:20 pm, we pulled into the Dallas bus terminal. My heart pounded thinking about seeing Cody. The bus was 20 minutes early. Cody was still on his way. Like every passenger on the bus, I held my pee rather than use that toilet. I rushed into the restroom and relieved myself. This restroom was clean, and there was nobody in there but one other cowboy. He was handsome - his body was big like he lifted a lot of bales of hay. I only glanced at him, but right away, he came over to where I was finishing up. I shook my dick and put it back in my pants. I was trying to save something of myself for Cody, and this guy was making it tough. He had a big bulge underneath his Texas Rangers belt buckle. I smiled and turned to walk away from him. He grabbed my hand and put it on his crotch. It felt funny.

"Look, Mister, I—"

The next thing I knew, he dragged me out in handcuffs.

"I didn't do nothing!" I shouted.

"What are you saying? Are you saying it was me?" He punched my jaw, and the lights went out.

I came to, staring up at a crowd of bus travelers, shaking their heads and judging me. Then I spied Cody.

"Cody! Help!"

Cody came running.

"What's going on here?" he demanded.

"This little faggot was waving his dick at me, and he grabbed my crotch!"

"Says who?"

"Says me." He pulled out a badge.

"Got any witnesses?" Cody put his hands on his hips. He towered over the police officer.

"No." The police officer was scared of the big cowboy. I could see it.

"Do you know who this is?"

The police officer shook his head.

"This is the number one bullfighter in the US. You're holding a legend in cuffs. We got an exhibition to get to and...."

"Fine." The cop undid my handcuffs.

Cody was still pissed at the cop.

"Now, apologize for calling Brightie Matthews a faggot."

Cody was so virile; he was in charge of the cop now.

"I'm sorry, Mr. Matthews."

I shocked Cody when I reached for the officer's

waistline. I stuck my hand in his polyester pants and pulled out a rolled-up sock.

"Apology accepted. And this isn't fooling anybody."

I could have ended up in jail, but I was so angry.

Cody took me by the arm and dragged me to the parking lot.

"Cody, I'm sorry, I just went in there to take a piss--"

"I know. That restroom is a war zone. You never know what you'll find in there. I know you didn't do anything."

I searched for Cody's truck, but he had a silver Corvette this time. It was an expensive car. There was more for me to learn about my cowboy lover.

✤ 21 ✤

MCKINNEY

On the road to McKinney, I put my head in Cody's lap, pretending to sleep. What I really wanted was a close-up view of his thigh and the big, genuine bulge running down it. Cody didn't need no sock.

Cody's house was a mansion. The front of his house wasn't a driveway; it was a circle with a fountain and plants growing out the middle. His house was like it was from Mexico. He told me it wasn't a mansion; it was a hacienda.

"What do your parents do?"

He laughed. "This is my place."

"What do I gotta do to get a place like this?"

Cody smiled. "Invest wisely."

I didn't know what that meant, but I pretended I did.

A Mexican butler came and took our luggage from the backseat. I followed him down a long stone pathway with pretty flowers and bushes cut in shapes. The front door was something a pirate would push open to go into a bar. Inside, I couldn't believe what I saw. The walls was white, but they reflected the sun like glass. I put one hand on the entryway wall.

"It's beeswax," Cody said. "I polish the plaster with beeswax to keep it dry."

"I didn't know you were Mexican."

"I'm not. What do you mean?"

"Well, I mean, you live in a Mexican house. I figured you must be Mexican."

Cody smiled and shook his head. "I just like this style. It stays cool in the summer and warm in the winter."

His house went on for miles. There was an upstairs, where the butler took me and my bags.

"I don't speak no Spanish, sir, but I hope you understand when I ask what's your name."

"I'm Diego. I grew up in Dallas."

"Oh, Diego, sorry. I wasn't sure."

Diego shrugged. He threw my bag next to Cody's on a big bed in a room the size of our house in Oklahoma. It had a television and radio built into the wall, three closet doors, and a door that went to the bathroom.

❧ 22 ❧

SQUEAKY CLEAN

The bathroom was covered in reddish-brown tiles. The sinks were blue and white; they matched the shower and the bathtub. He had both!

Cody came up behind me and wrapped me in his arms. It felt so good, so safe. There was something big throbbing in his jeans. I couldn't wait. But Cody wanted something first. He brought out a red rubber hot water bottle with a white tube coming out of it.

"What's that"?

"It's an enema. It's to wash you on the inside. He turned on the shower. There was room for both of us. There were six shower heads pointing all over the place.

While I soaped up, Cody added warm water to the rubber bottle. He hung it with a hook from the highest nozzle. He pinched the tube and lowered the end, which had a plastic nozzle. Cody spat on it and stuck it up my butt.

"You won't notice anything but warmth for a few seconds. As soon as you feel pressure, tap my arm." He let go of the tube, and water came pouring in.

It was a lot like the time Cody pissed up my ass. The warm stream felt so good. Then all of a sudden, I had to poop real bad. I tapped Cody, and he put a kink in the tube.

"Do I have to hold it?" I was gonna explode all over Cody's nice shower.

Cody pointed to the toilet. I didn't need no further instructions. I sat on the pot and released it all. It took a lot longer to come out than it did to go in. My tummy was having spasms. After a few minutes, it calmed back down. Cody motioned for me to join him in the shower again. He put the nozzle up my butt again and released water. I tapped him again. It was like I was at the Doctor's office.

This time it was water that came out, but I was surprised to see it was still brown. How dirty was I?

This time, Cody inspected the bowl before he let me flush it.

"Definitely another."

The third batch was clear until the last squeeze, which came out brown.

Cody nodded. He refilled the bag with fresh water and told me this time, I was to stay in the shower. He asked me to let him know when it was uncomfortable. I did, but he smiled and kept going. To my surprise, the discomfort didn't get any worse. He let the whole bag fill me up.

"You can just let it go when you're ready."

My tummy was twitching bad. "But I'll get it all over you."

"It's just water now." I didn't have time to make it to the toilet now.

"Just push it all out in one go."

Cody turned me so my ass was pointed right at his waist. I couldn't hold it. I opened my butthole and pushed with all my might. Cody played with himself. It didn't take long this time. The water was clear. Cody bent down and put his face in the stream. And then it was over.

"Can you handle another one?"

I nodded. This time, Cody kept the bag under the shower head, so more and more water went way up. I felt my belly. It was swollen as a cow udder. Cody rubbed it and smiled like a proud father.

Finally, the pressure was too painful. I tapped Cody, who pulled the nozzle out and signaled for me to wait. This was uncomfortable. Cody took his halfway-hard dick and rubbed it up against my butthole. Thank God he didn't try to put it in. He gave the go-ahead, and I sprayed warm water all over his dick and balls. Again, Cody bent down to wash his face in my butt shower. When it was out, he turned the nozzles up to hot. The shower filled with steam.

He lathered my whole body, even in places I never thought to wash. The six nozzles washed away all the soap in seconds.

I'd never been so clean. It was humbling to see all that gunk that had been hiding out inside me. It was good to be rid of it.

☙ 23 ❧

ASS OLYMPICS

After I dried off, Cody showed me to the bedroom. He dropped to one knee and started licking my ass. His tongue was stretching me and slicking up my insides.

Next, I felt a cold glob of Albolene and heard Cody rubbing himself. I turned and caught a glimpse of his cock. It was all the way hard and bigger than I remembered. It was a few weeks we were apart; I'd wager he couldn't find no pleasure from anybody. Not like I could. I understood why his dick looked so needy as it did. I was the only one who could keep Cody from sinning with his hands.

It always hurt some when Cody put it in me. Nothing like the first time, but it started out painful every time we did it up in Laramie. I found out that it's like an Olympic sport. You gotta always be in training for it; then it won't hurt so much. Right then, when the top of the Louisville Slugger crawled up my shitter, it felt like the very first time. The only difference was I knew it would stop hurting and feel real good soon enough. He pushed back against the inside door. Turning that corner was worse than anything I felt today. I was glad Cody was behind me so that he couldn't see my face. I did my best to make noises that encouraged him. I was afraid they would come out in screams.

After two terrible minutes, during which I wondered if I should call an ambulance, my ass started to remember Cody and how good he was at fucking me. I pushed my hips toward him, trying to squeeze every single inch of him up in my guts. His pubic hairs tickled my buttcheeks as he came in for a landing. His hips squished my butt. Two or three inches of him still weren't inside me.

Cody read my mind. He picked me up and lay me on my side, lifting one of my legs over his shoulder. That angle gave him a straight trail into me. My eyes fluttered when he pushed forward two more inches, and I moaned. His balls were touching my butthole. He was all the way in.

After that, he didn't waste no time. He took short, fast strokes like a jackhammer. His big balls slammed into mine. I rolled my head so I could see his handsome face. He lifted me so's he could kiss me. When his tongue met mine, it felt like we was on the Ferris wheel going down. I got goosebumps. My dick leaked a spoonful of that clear stuff. Cody caught it and ate it. It made me feel wanted and valuable when he did that.

"Brightie, it's been too long for me. I can't hold back."

"Fill me up. Give me a Cody enema."

Those words were like a magic spell because he let loose with a flood of his cum. It felt a lot like an enema. My body tried to push it out, but Cody's dick was like a cork. He was still hard.

I could honestly say that Cody's huge dick felt downright comfortable inside me. I thought the next time wouldn't hurt one bit. I was right because Cody pumped back and forth again. He was going for round two. It was perfect, like his giant cock belonged inside me. There was no pain or hurt, just a pleasure that had to be the reason God put man on Earth, to know paradise. Cody sat me on his lap, facing him, another good angle to take him all the way. He stood up and carried me around the giant bedroom, holding me up against the walls when he needed a rest. We tried a bunch of positions, but we came back to me on my side with a leg over his shoulder. This time, I saw my stomach moving in rhythm to Cody's fucking. That was his dick pushing organs out of the way.

That put me over the top. Thinking about this man who had the power to rearrange my insides, and all the pleasure he got from doing it, and how I was the only one on Earth he ever met who could handle it...it started with a heavy flow of the clear sticky stuff. Cody scooped it up and swallowed it. He leaned in and whispered, "Kid, I think I love you." That was what did it. He's fucking me, and he loves me, and he's got this big mansion and a great big cock, and that's right - he loves me, and we're flying to Brazil...it all came together at once. My pecker had been throbbing, but now it was pulling back like a cannon about to fire. Cody pulled my trigger when he said. "Oh shit, I'm gonna come."

I beat him to it. My whole body shook, then the sperm came sailing out of me.

When Cody saw me do that without hands, he shook his head like a whinnying horse and bellowed, "Fuck, Brightie! I'm coming! I'm coming!" And come he did. More pressure built up behind his bung plug of a cockhead. There was a white river rising.

When Cody's cock softened, and I pushed him out, it was followed by a few weeks' worth of saved-up sperm. It formed a small pond on the bedspread. Cody fed me some and took some for himself before he cleaned it up. My come had shot so hard and far, we didn't find it then. Later, it dripped off the ceiling fan and landed on Cody's neck. We both laughed.

For someone who couldn't do it until he met me,

Cody was already an expert. Of course, I never done it before we met, so we were both finding out new stuff. None of the others I'd been with were anything like him. The First Clown with the big furry thighs in the middle of that cowboy pile-on was the best besides Cody, but he weren't even a close contender. Cody was the best at everything he did. He didn't always win the competition but was the best competitor in looks and style.

I put an arm across his chest and listened to his breath. He was still winded from that last ride.

MEXICAN FOOD AND
DESSERT

Somebody knocked. I panicked, searching for my clothes, but Cody patted me to calm me down.

"Is that you, Diego?"

"Yes, sir. Maria asked me to tell you that dinner will be ready in 10 minutes."

"Thank you." Cody stood and pulled on his skin-tight jeans and a cowboy shirt. He reached into my bag and laid out a pair of jeans and my favorite embroidered cowboy shirt with imitation pearl snaps.

"I hope you like Mexican food, Brightie."

"We don't have none in Clinton. Unless you count tamales from a can."

"This is a lot different. We're having ceviche as an appetizer and enchiladas verdes for the main course."

I didn't know what that was, but I didn't want to be rude and turn it down.

Ceviche turned out to be a big glass goblet with raw seafood in lemon juice. It comes with these flat crispy corn cakes called tostadas, and you eat it with avocado. It sounded disgusting, and it smelled worse, but it tasted real good. It was spicy, like Tabasco sauce but with a different flavor. Maria even gave me a bottle of Tabasco in case I wanted to add it, but I only ever put that stuff on my grits. I like the way it burns.

Next, she brought out the enchiladas verdes. They were made from a soft, flat corn cake, white melted cheese, chicken, and this tangy green sauce that made my mouth water. Cody told me the soft corn cakes are called tortillas, and when you fry them crisp, they're tostadas. They served mushed-up pinto beans and orange rice on the side. I cleaned my plate. It made Maria smile. Cody was glad he introduced me to new food that I liked.

We went up to Cody's bedroom for a good night's sleep. Neither of us was tired, so we watched TV until we couldn't stand it no more, and sure enough, we was back kissing. Kissing made us both hard, and that turned into even more sex.

This time, Cody took me and put me inside him with nothing but spit. He pounded the bedsheets and cried from the pain, but I didn't feel sorry for him. I knew my dick could never hurt a person like his did. I fucked him face down. I loved staring at the white hills of his butt and how my fat dick pushed its way between them. When I pulled out all the way, I loved watching Cody's butthole go from a big hollow circle to a little pink eye. I wondered if he did that with me, and if so, how big that circle became, and if it ever even closed. I made a game of spitting into the open circle before it closed up. It had the added benefit of making it smoother fucking for Cody, the crybaby. I put my hands on his butt and wiggled the muscles so that they slapped the sides of my dick. Oh man, that was good. I kept at it.

Cody said, "Yeah, Yeah, play with my ass." So I kept at it.

"Slap it, Brightie." So I slapped it, which startled me because it made his hole close tight for a second. If I kept a rhythm, I could slap his ass on the outstroke, and he'd tighten up on the instroke. Every third thrust, wham! I walloped him on the ass. The way I was moving at such an even pace, and the slapping of Cody's beautiful butt, set the wheels in motion. I felt my dick leak inside Cody. He must have felt it. I wanted him to come at the same time as me. I reached down and found his nipple pressed against the bedsheet. I played with it. He bucked like a bronco. I kept my steady pace and slapped with one hand, tweaked with the other. Cody moaned.

"You like when your little clown smacks your ass!"

"Yes, Brightie, slap it harder!"

I didn't hold back. I gave a smack that was gonna leave a mark. Cody cried out, but it wasn't pain. His butthole clenched so tight that it could have broken my dick. That felt good, so I kept wailing on his ass, letting his butthole squeeze my cock.

About ten slaps in, I heard Cody whisper, "You're making me come."

He was playing with himself near the base, but his dick was so long it came out from under him. The head was aimed skyward. Cody shot white cream in my eye and on my bare chest. I pounded hard, forgetting the pace, and slapped Cody's ass viciously with both hands until I recognized that tingling below my belly button.

"You ready for it?"

"Yes. Come in me!" Cody didn't have to beg twice. As if it weren't the third time today, I painted his insides white with a huge load of cum. When I pulled out, his ass was gaping open, and a stream of my cum drained out of him, bigger than any load today. I caught what I could in my palm and fed it to Cody. He grunted like a pig when he lapped up my sperm.

Afterward, both of us was sweaty and gasping for air. I remember in school, when I learned a new sport, I never was good at it from the start, not like some of the guys. But as I kept at it, I got better. And the guys who were good from the start didn't get much better. That's what it was like having sex with Cody. We both started off scared and unsure of what we were doing. Cody knew a lot more, but he still had some firsts. That day we were both like experts.

He took my hand. "Brightie, I'm sure gonna love being in Brazil with you."

"Me too. Do you know if they have Mexican food there?" Cody laughed again real hard to the point I was almost ashamed. He took my head in his hands and kissed me. It took me a minute to kiss back, but I did. Maybe I shouldn't have because it caused both of us to go hard again.

We tried to fall asleep, but we were both hard and needed to do something about it.

So we gave in and went for yet another round. This time, Cody wanted to try something different he called "sixty-nine." He flipped so each of our heads was facing the other's crotch. We stayed in that position, sucking on each other's cocks. It was a long time before I tasted salt in Cody's dick. Once I did, my own dick squirted out some of that clear stuff. Two minutes later, we gave each other the last creamy meal of the day. Dessert, but it wasn't ice cream. It was past midnight when we both drifted off to sleep.

✻ 25 ✻

FEAR OF FLYING

Our flight to Houston was scheduled to leave at 11:00 am. You can take the boy off the farm, but you can't take the farm out of the boy. We were up at the crack of dawn. Back home, it was our neighbor's rooster that woke me every morning. Here, it was just being next to Cody when his arm hair brushed up against mine. That's all I needed.

Maria made scrambled eggs with tomatoes, onions, and hot green peppers. She gave me steamy fresh tortillas instead of toast and no butter. The plate had more of those mashed beans and half an avocado. No bacon, no sausage. But it was still delicious.

Corvettes get stolen a lot, so Cody decided to drive his truck to the airport. Dallas Love Airport is right in the middle of town. Cody told me that it used to be the outskirts of Dallas, but the city grew up around it.

The stewardess escorted us to our seats at the front of the plane. As soon as we sat, I put my seat belt on.

I didn't want to admit it, but I was afraid to fly. I just couldn't believe those heavy hunks of metal could stay in the air, all filled up with passengers. As it got closer to 11:00, I was soaked in sweat. I didn't want Cody to see, but he did.

"Brightie, are you all right?" He put a hand on my wet forehead, but it was cold, not hot.

"Yeah, Cody, everything's cool." I hoped that was enough, but it wasn't.

"You're all cold and clammy. What's wrong?"

Damn him. He knew me too well. "I'm not sure I believe that airplanes can fly. I can't understand why they don't just fall."

I thought he was gonna laugh at me, but instead, he hugged me. "I never heard someone describe the fear of flying so well." He let me go. "You know, for my work, I fly a lot. I think I must have flown a hundred times or more. And never once did we even come close to falling."

"Where do you fly?"

"Mostly New York, Toronto, and Tulsa."

I wondered what he did on those trips. Who he saw, who he gave his ass to. Whose dick he sucked. I was jealous of his lovers.

I glanced over my shoulder, but most of the plane was curtained off. There were maybe ten of us in our little section. It was weird.

"Why are there people behind that curtain?"

"We're in first class. I upgraded us."

The stewardess brought us both stiff drinks. Mine was bourbon and ginger ale. I gulped it down. It worked a little. I was still scared.

When we took off, I might have wet my pants a tiny bit. It wasn't right or natural to be sitting at a 30-degree angle. Gravity wasn't right. Maybe that's why the airplane floats. I opened the curtain and saw Dallas sprawling below us. It was so far down. It wasn't real anymore; I couldn't stay scared when whatever we was gonna crash into was so far below.

Cody put one of his big hands over mine and smiled. In a while, the plane leveled off. Then not twenty minutes later, we pointed down, and I freaked out again.

The captain announced we were descending to Hobby Airport in Houston. Another fifteen minutes went by, and then we hit the ground hard. It was the scaredest I've ever been. But everyone else stayed calm. I heard a noise like the engines was about to blow up.

"Cody, what's that?"

"They reversed the propellers. It makes a lot of noise. Totally normal."

His hand was still on mine. I realized he had it there the whole flight. How could somebody be so caring and friendly to a stupid clown like me? I was lucky to have him near me. It made me want to keep him near me. That had to be love. It felt so warm and safe.

✤ 26 ✤
BAG BOY

At Hobby, we had to switch to Pan Am for the next leg of our flight – Lima, Peru. We waited while a big dopey baggage boy in a uniform brought our bags and put them on a countertop. We had to wait until every bag was in place, then we lined up, showed him our ticket, and he gave us the bag. He had a face like a monkey but was somehow good-looking. I smiled as I collected my luggage, and he smiled right back. Cody didn't miss anything.

"You like him, eh?"

I blushed. "He's alright."

"He likes you. He's one of ours. Look."

The monkey-faced baggage boy was done handing out bags. He stood staring at me, rubbing his crotch right out there in the airport. Why was he looking at me and not Cody? I wasn't nothing special.

Cody nudged me. "Go on, go talk to him."

"Don't we have a plane to catch?"

"In three hours. Go have fun, Brightie."

My feelings were hurt. Cody wanted me to do it with somebody else. He put his hand on my back. He didn't exactly push me, but he made it so it would be much easier to walk toward the monkey boy than stay where I was.

I gave in and walked up to him. He was still rubbing his crotch and staring at mine.

"Where you flying?" he asked me.

"Brazil."

He whistled. "That your Dad?"

"No. We're, um, friends."

"Fuck buddies, am I right?"

"I guess." I didn't like that term, but it was accurate.

"Did he just loan you out to me?"

I turned red. It wasn't this guy that was making me angry. It was his words and how correct they were. Fuck it. "Yeah, he did." In my head, I shrugged. I stopped fighting.

"What you into?" He walked out on the tarmac, and I followed.

"Sex."

He laughed. "Yeah, me too. Come on."

The baggage boy led me into an employee restroom. It was empty. He locked the door.

"You want I fuck you? Or you wanna fuck me?"

I thought out loud. "My friend is so big, I probably wouldn't even feel you inside me."

Bam! Baggage boy punched my jaw.

"You think so, Blondie? I'll make you beg for more."

He was rough. He pushed me to my knees and took out his dick. It was definitely big, but it wasn't huge. I was bigger. He pushed his way into my mouth and part-way down my throat. It was as easy as walking down the street.

"Why ain't you choking?"

My mouth was full, so I shrugged. He pulled out. "You're doing it wrong."

"You never let me finish. I wanna fuck you."

He pulled his coveralls down and showed me a prize-winning rump.

"Now that's what I'm talking about. You ready?"

He pulled some Vaseline out of his pants pocket and

fingered his butthole to make it slippery. I did him a favor and spat on my dick before pushing my way in.

"Fuuuck! Ow! Damn, Blondie, take it easy."

"Shut up, Bag Boy." He punched me, and I was gonna make him regret it. Once my head was in, I pushed all the way. Monkey Boy shrieked.

"Ow! Fuck! Ooooooooowwww! You motherfucker!"

"Watch your language." The tension broke, and we both laughed. Sex without laughter is dull.

"You're huge, dude. I thought I was big."

"I'm nothing compared to my friend."

Enough talking. I stared at the peach fuzz on the baggage handler's ass. It was so fuzzy I had to run my hand over it, not touching his beautiful butt, just grazing the hairs. I was fucking him hard, but he wouldn't let me turn the corner, so I kept bouncing off the back of his ass.

"Oh! Ow! Oh!" he didn't like me punching him there.

"Let me in, man."

"What do you mean?" I found it hard to believe this man didn't know as much as me.

"You know, the inner door. Open up." I pushed against it, but it didn't yield.

"Ow! Fuck!" He was upset. "What are you talking about?"

I kept pushing and corrected his angle; then I slipped right through. "There," I said.

"Oh god, oh my fucking god. Did you poke a hole? What is, ohhhhh! Fuck that's good!"

I waited for him to acclimatize to my dick all the way in him. "Let me know when you're ready, bag boy."

"Oh god, it's so good. Please fuck me hard! Now!" He sounded like he was about to pass out.

I punched, poked, and plowed his ass as hard and fast as I could. It was obvious he had never been with someone big like me. Imagine if Cody were here.

The monkey-faced bag boy was leaking the clear sticky fluid. I caught some in my hand. He turned to look at me while I licked it up.

"Are you eating my pre-cum? That's disgusting."

So that's what it was called. I gathered more in my hand and held it up to his mouth. He refused it.

I insisted. "Eat it!"

Between his moans, he obeyed. He licked my hand clean. He grabbed his dick and pulled on it. It's a sin, but He is the judge, not me.

I wondered if smacking his ass would cause him to clench. I smacked him. He clenched.

We switched to a more comfortable position. He sat on the toilet with his coveralls off, and I plowed him from the front. He pulled on his dick hard and used his other hand to bring my lips to his. Kissing had a magic effect on me. I grew bigger and longer. I went deeper. His eyes opened wide, and he pulled away.

"Goddamn, dude, you're gonna split me in two!"

I guess I was pretty big if Cody were not counted. I pulled the boy's hips so they hung off the toilet and put my hands on the wall. This let me go as deep as possible in an employee restroom. His legs shook, and his stroking reached a fever pace. He spat in his hand and made it slippery so he could stroke without getting an Indian burn.

"Blondie, you did it. I'm gonna-- I'm gonna fucking--" I held his hand still.

He knew without asking. With his other hand, he pinched my teat. It was electric. My belly filled with warm tingling. I let go of his hand. He spat again and stroked himself like a locomotive.

"Yeeeeeeeahhh." He was close.

I said, "Oh, man, oh, keep pinching."

I changed to long strokes, so I nearly exited him and then plunged way past his inner door. He had this surprised look like someone had pulled a gun on him. But it wasn't fear.

He threw his head back. "Fuck yeah. Fuck yeah. Fuck yeah. Oh god, oh god, you're so bi-i-i-g. Oh, Jesus. Oh, sweet Jesus."

And after taking our Lord's name in vain, he sprayed me with come.

I was close. I took ten more long strokes, then switched back to small strokes that let my head move in and out of the inner door. That surprised expression never left the monkey boy's face. He pulled me to his lips and kissed me. That was the magic bullet.

"Oh. Get ready, guy. You ready?"

He nodded.

"O-o-o-o-o-o-o-h-h-h!" My balls emptied into him. I kept at it until I had milked every drop from my big penis.

I stayed buried inside him, but he pushed my hips.

"It hurts now; I came." He complained.

So still hard, I pulled out of him. I let the last of my cum dribble out of my dick onto the floor in front of the toilet. The luggage handler farted my cum into the toilet. He didn't bother flushing or wiping.

He was covered in sweat and semen but didn't even take a paper towel. He just put his coveralls back on.

We kissed, then he said, "Twenty-five."

"What?"

"Twenty-five dollars."

I was stupefied. He was charging me for the best sex of his fucking life. Was all that moaning and talk about me being huge just whore talk? My heart ached.

He laughed. "Just kidding. Man, you should have seen your face. Crazy."

It took me a few seconds to switch gears. I was mad, but I know he thought it was funny. Just to release the tension, I punched him in the arm.

"Yep, you had me there."

There was a loud bang on the door. "Goddamnit, Tony, you been in there for hours! I gotta shit!"

He unlocked the door. I was terrified to be caught. But the negro who walked in gave me half a glance.

"Passenger emergency," Tony said.

"Hunh. Get the fuck out." The angry man pointed to the door. We left quickly. Tony (I assume he was Tony) ushered me back into the airport. Cody was waiting in a leather chair.

I turned to say thanks or goodbye, but the bag boy was already two gates away.

❧ 27 ❧

NONSTOP TO LIMA

"You look like the cat that ate the canary." Cody ribbed me.

"I'm no cat, and I didn't eat that bird."

"Did you make a sausage roll on a white bun?"

I snorted. "Hold the mustard, extra mayo." Despite my cheating ways, I was jealous of Cody. 'What about you? Eat any birds?"

He smiled. "There's one bathroom, and they got holes in the stall walls. I would never fit through one of them, but I might have had a small bird or two."

I was seething with jealousy, but I kept it inside. How did Cody do it? He pimped me out to that baggage handler. Didn't he get jealous? I vowed to find out.

Our plane to Lima was much bigger. First Class was full. Everybody dressed rich. All the ladies wore pearl necklaces and white gloves. The men all had fancy fedoras and suits. I would have felt underdressed in my jeans and cowboy boots if Cody weren't dressed the same.

"Everybody's so fancy," I whispered.

"We're rodeo. We're dressed just how we should be." Cody had more experience, so I trusted his judgment.

Sure enough, after we had been flying for a few hours and folks had gone to sleep, one husky businessman across the aisle from Cody leaned in and asked, "What's a couple of cowboys like you doing on a flight to Lima?"

"Rodeo in Brazil."

The man was impressed. He had a hundred questions. Cody wasn't just being polite. He was seducing this man. I heard it in his answers.

"You ride a bull for a living?"

"I ride...bulls, yes."

"What's it like?" The businessman leaned in close.

"It's a rough ride, but it always ends smoothly."

The businessman was polite. "I'm Harry. Harry Sanders."

"Cody, and this here's Brightie." When I took the businessman's hand, it was soft and cool. His nails were cut and polished. His cufflinks had to be genuine diamonds.

"I'm only going as far as Lima. Boy, I wish I could see you boys ride."

Cody was shameless. "It's quite a sight when we ride. Even better to feel that thrill of the bull smacking into you."

The businessman touched his crotch. Nothing obvious, just a quick adjustment. Cody went in for the kill.

"If you want to see what me and Brightie can do, just ask." Cody nodded toward the bathrooms at the front of the plane.

Harry rubbed his crotch hard. "I'd like that. I'd like that very much."

Cody stood abruptly and entered one of the bathrooms. Harry followed, entering the same lavatory. I was sad, mad, and frustrated, until Cody leaned out and motioned me to come.

Cody took up most of that bathroom, so he sat on the toilet. The businessman faced Cody and gave his butt to me. Cody removed the man's trousers and underwear. I left my belt buckled, but I unbuttoned my jeans. My dick was still a little greasy from my adventure with Tony.

Cody had already taken Harry into his mouth. I studied the husky man's butt and thighs. He wasn't fat - he was muscled. The muscles spread up his waist into his upper body, which was covered by his suit coat, vest, and dress shirt. I moved all those layers up as high as possible to show what he was packing. He was a weightlifter, for sure. He had a V-shape made from his incredible wing muscles and small waist. I rubbed the edges of the V, surprised that the skin was as soft as his hands. I kissed his wing muscles, his armpits, his back, the little indentations near the base of his spine, and his massive butt cheeks. He was gifted with a huge ass, bigger than Cody's. I spent a long time there before I kissed his inner thigh. From there, I could see Cody's mustache. He quickly swallowed Harry, who was small down there. As I kissed the bodybuilder, I was impressed by how soft all of his skin was. Cody had rough skin like you'd expect from a bull rider. Harry was like satin. I returned to his beautiful mounds of butt flesh. I parted them and pressed my lips towards his pink butthole. I wedged my tongue pretty far up inside him and made sure he was well-prepared for me. I stood and spit on my dick. Harry reached behind him and found it. He pulled me close.

"Damn, boy, that's a huge pecker."

"You should see Cody's." I wish I hadn't said that. That dick was my property as far as I was concerned.

Harry guided me to his hole. It was pretty hard to find at the bottom of that beautiful valley. It was good that I had a few extra inches because I couldn't even reach the back of his butthole from this angle. Harry was shorter than me. I motioned him to put his leg up on the sink. His hole was exposed. Cody was playing with his tiny balls. My height gave me another four inches or so to dig into Harry. I reached the back and kept going. Either he'd had big ones before, or the leg on the sink opened that inner door. He moaned when I passed through it, but he didn't scream or freak out. He tilted his hips back and forth, massaging my cock. I was pressed against the restroom door so I couldn't thrust in that direction. While Harry rocked back and forth, I bent and straightened my legs. It worked.

Harry got curious about Cody's dick. He undid my man's jeans and reached in. He couldn't extract the cock because Cody was rock hard. The businessman traced the outline and gasped. He turned to me.

"Does he fuck you with that?" It was weird to talk about Cody like he was a cow for sale. Cody just kept sucking on Harry's little dick. He wasn't bothered, so why should I be?

"Yeah, he does."

"Holy fuck. Stop." He stopped tickling my dick with his butt and pulled out of Cody's mouth.

"You said you would show me what you guys could do. I want to see that." I exchanged glances with Cody to get a feel for what he wanted. Harry misinterpreted our pause.

"Oh, I'll pay you well. It will be worth your while."

Cody smirked. He didn't need money. This was just a question of privacy. He spoke first.

"We gotta switch positions to make it work."

Harry took charge. "I want to jack off watching you, so I'll take the door."

After a bit of reshuffling, I faced Harry, my ass at Cody's eye level. Cody lowered his jeans to release the monster. Harry was so shocked, he lost his balance. "Jesus H. Christ."

I dropped my jeans to my ankles. Cody took out a small tube of Albolene and applied it to his cock and my ass. Practice makes perfect. A little spit, and I slid down the length of Cody's pole like a fireman. Harry pounded away at his little penis. "Holy fuck." he whispered.

I kept going, passing the door and deep into my belly.

Harry hissed, "I can see it in you. Right there." He pointed to the bump on my belly as I bounced up and down on the flesh baseball bat.

I felt rain. Harry had just shot his wad.

"I got another in me. Keep going."

I leaned back and kissed Cody on the mouth. In front of the witness, I said, "I love you."

Cody responded quickly, "I love you, too, Brightie."

Harry's fist was a blur. "Oh god, you two are so hot."

Cody put both hands on my nipples. I released some pre-cum. Harry caught it and licked it up. He put his mouth on my penis but didn't go deep. I realized I was too thick for his little mouth. After a great struggle, he popped the head in and moved it to the back of his throat.

Cody kept at my nipples.

I wanted Cody to come inside me. I reached back and played with his nipples. It was uncomfortable, but it was the shortcut. I was ready to come in Harry's mouth, but he spat me out, turned, and sat on my cock. I was stuffed by Cody behind me and stuffing Harry's round, muscled ass in front. I was like a Tinkertoy spool.

I heard Cody's breath quicken. He moved my hands away from his nipples. Just knowing he was going to shoot inside me put me past the edge. We had to all be quiet, but our moans and grunts were reaching a peak. Cody was first.

"Unnnnhhh. Oh, Brightie, Oh Brightie. Oooooooh. Yeah!" Cody's load filled my belly. That sent me over. My insides were stuffed with Cody's flesh and coated in his semen. I shot into Harry's big round butt.

"Mm-mm-mm-mm-yeah-mm-mm." I sounded like a

girl, but I didn't care. I slapped Harry's ass, and he pinched the last drops of semen out of my pecker.

Harry was silent, but we both saw him shudder and heard his second batch of semen fall to the floor in loud drops.

Harry was the first to dress and leave. He left five one-hundred-dollar bills on the tiny sink. I was about to say something, but Cody held my wrist, putting a finger to his lips.

Alone in the bathroom, I wanted to talk to Cody about all these men in our bed, so to speak.

Cody was nearly dressed. I was still naked from the waist down. I needed more room to reach my pants!

"Cody, can I talk to you about something?"

"Yeah, Brightie, of course. Is everything okay?"

"It will be after we talk. See, I want to talk about our, uh, experiences with other men."

"In the past?"

"And now and the future. I'm confused. I thought we loved each other."

"Brightie, I love you with all my heart. No one could ever take the place of you."

"Then why do you put people between us?"

"Oh, I see. Were your mom and pop faithful?"

"Yes. Until he died of scarlet fever."

"So you think love means being faithful."

"Well, yes, the Bible says—"

Cody interrupted, "That we're abominations. Don't worry about the Bible."

"But isn't it adultery?"

"No. First, we're not married and never could be. Second, since we can't get married, we're not held to the same rules. We can have fun. No kids end up hurt. Do you follow?"

I didn't, exactly. 'Well, won't we end up hurting each other?"

"Only if we stop loving one another. As long as we

love each other, nothing can separate us. Not sex, nothing."

"But the Bible says some other stuff about this." I was torn up.

"A lot of the Bible is out of date. Let's stick to Jesus, who, after all, is the living God that we all answer to. What did Jesus say is the highest law, above all others?"

"To love each other."

"Exactly. As long as we love each other, we're good."

"It still is weird."

"You're new to love, Brightie. I lost someone I loved and didn't think I would love again until I met you." I wondered who he had lost; I didn't want to pry.

"I'm a lot better, Cody. I'm not all the way there, and I feel awful jealous, but I think I accept most of it."

When we were dressed, we opened the door to find a stewardess standing there with her hands on her hips.

Cody didn't miss a beat. "We had a private discussion. An argument, really."

"Oh, okay." She let us go back to our seats as easy as that.

Cody drifted right off to sleep. Harry smiled at me. He handed me a little clear plastic bag sealed with cello tape. "A gift from my company," he said.

"What is it?"

"Joy powder. Don't take it to Brazil."

❧ 28 ❧

JOY POWDER

I woke up when the plane smacked into the runway. Before I had time to be scared, we slowed down and taxied towards the Lima terminal. When the plane stopped, Harry put his suitcase on the ground, like he needed something, but he didn't. He just wanted to tease me with his big round ass. Cody licked his lips, admiring the muscleman's perfect behind.

I said, "Cody, if you wanted to, I wouldn't mind."

Harry interrupted, "Hell no. I know my limits, and your man is way beyond."

The sorrow in Cody's eyes about near broke my heart. Finally, the little metal staircase rolled up, and we climbed out of the plane. We had six hours until our flight to Sao Paulo.

Harry gave us each a hug and made sure to let us know he had muscles.

"Enjoy the rest of your trip. Oh, and remember, don't take the joy powder to Brazil." Harry walked away, ass wiggling below his V-shaped torso.

Cody frowned. "Joy powder?"

I reached into my front pocket and showed him. "It's a gift from Harry's company."

He snatched it from my hands and put it in his

cowboy boot. "We shouldn't be seen with this cocaine. We need to throw it away."

Cocaine? I had heard a little about it from out-of-town clowns. It sounded dangerous. Why would a nice guy like Harry give that to us?

Cody took me to the Pan Am First Class Lounge. It was like a country club in a Hollywood Movie. I didn't know what the people did, but they made a lot of money doing it.

Cody sat down in a plush leather chair, reached into his boot, and casually dropped the bag on the ground. He checked that nobody saw, then said, "I gotta call New York. I'll be right over there. He pointed to a business office with a secretary.

"Oh, you gotta talk to New York. What time is it there?"

Cody pointed to a row of clocks. New York was 9:30 am. We were at 8:30.

"This is first class, so have fun, Brightie."

The secretary stood and welcomed him. She sat him at a desk with a phone and helped him dial.

There was a tap on my shoulder. It was the waiter.

"Can I get you anything, sir?" He spoke with a thick accent, but he spoke way more English than I did Spanish or any other language. "We have full English Breakfast, Cheese Omelet, or Traditional Peruvian Breakfast. Oh, and your friend dropped this." He smiled and handed me the cocaine.

I looked up and saw him for the first time. Holy shit! He was not what I expected to see. He was tall, pale, with curly brown hair and dark blue eyes. His smile could melt the ice in your drink.

"Do you want it?" I tried to hand it back to him. He put his hand over mine.

"Don't you?"

I blushed. "I don't know what to do with it."

The waiter's smile brightened. "Come. I show you."

He took me through the double doors to the kitchen and down a long dark hallway to an office. He unlocked the door and ushered me in, locking us in after.

He poured some of the white powder onto the desk. He took a playing card and broke the powder lumps apart. Then he arranged it into four short lines.

"I go first and show you." He took a Peruvian Sol out of his wallet and rolled it up. He covered one nostril and used the Sol to sniff one whole line into his other nostril. He switched sides and did the same.

When he stood up, his eyes were watering. He took a deep sniff and wiped at his nose.

"Your turn."

As a rodeo clown, I don't back down from a challenge. I was scared shitless, but I didn't want to let the waiter know. I snuffed the first line, then the second, and felt nothing.

I stood up, and the waiter smiled, leaning in to kiss me. My throat was numb. Soon my whole mouth was numb from the cocaine. Kissing this guy was good, then great, then the best fucking thing that ever existed or ever will exist.

I pulled away to admire his handsome face.

"I'm Brightie."

"Brightie. I'm Francisco." Within seconds, his pants were down at his ankles, and I got an eyeful of his nice-sized penis. It wasn't huge, not quite big. It was like medium-large. I dropped to my knees and opened my mouth, but he waggled a finger to stop me. Oh shit, he's not into other guys? Why did he pull it out?

My question was answered immediately. He tapped out some cocaine onto the widest part of his dick. I sniffed it off. Then he put it in my mouth. My whole throat and mouth were numbed by the coke still stuck to his dick. I saw him in my mouth but felt too good and numb to suck him. No problem. He held my head and humped my throat. It wasn't the first time I ever had a cock in my throat, but still, I didn't feel a need to throw up even a little bit. I just kept getting happier and happier for no reason. He came in my mouth. I only knew because some dribbled out of the corners.

He lifted me to him and sucked his own come out of my mouth. I felt his hands unbuckle my belt; my jeans fell to the ground. When he kneeled and pulled down my undershorts, the head of my cock smacked his chin.

"Oh!!" He was surprised by something.

"What?"

"You are so big!"

I shrugged. I knew I was nothing compared to Cody. He poured a lot of cocaine onto my dick.

"I need more to be able to relax." It made sense to me. Francisco took a huge whiff and cleared off most of the cocaine from my hard dick. Then he switched nostrils and finished off the rest. His eyes went hazy. With a great deal of difficulty, he took me in his mouth. He spent a minute or two getting used to that before he pushed me down his throat. After that, it was a blur. I know I came in his mouth. I know we kissed. I know the bag of cocaine was empty. I'm sure that a lot of the coke went on our dicks. I'm pretty sure we only had sex in the mouth because my butt was dry. I know at some point, I crashed a car in my head. There was no more cocaine. I think I cried.

FRANCISCO'S NO PRO

F rancisco led me out of the office and sent me back to my chair. Cody was still waiting for a line to New York.

How did all that happen so fast? Then I realized it could take two or three hours to get through from South America. Francisco offered me lunch instead. I had a Peruvian chicken sandwich with French fries. It was a lot like the sandwich at Top Hat but smelled better.

Francisco gave me special attention even after Cody returned from his phone call. He brought us a bottle of scotch for the trip to Brazil. The Embraer flight doesn't have American or European liquor - just South American. I was in a foul mood. I later learned that it was the cocaine that did that.

Francisco put hot towels on our necks; Cody wasn't expecting it. When Cody jumped, the waiter's eyes popped out of his head. He must have figured out what Cody had "in his pocket." Cody appreciated Francisco's service, and I could tell he was charmed by that smile. So it was no surprise when he adjusted himself to allow Francisco a better view of his manhood. I might have been okay with it if I wasn't so cranky. But I felt like crap, and I wanted Francisco to back off. I knew it wasn't fair, but that's how I felt.

When Cody went to the bathroom, and Francisco followed, I couldn't just sit there and take it. I snuck into the bathroom to spy on them.

Cody was peeing into the trough. Francisco undid his trousers and showed his nice-sized dick. Cody shook off the last drops, smiled, and went down on his knees. Francisco leaned his head back and let my man bring him to orgasm. He was fast. When Cody stood, Francisco shook his head. Cody shrugged, familiar with the rejection. That was enough. I broke my cover and crawled to Cody, pushing Francisco out of the way.

Cody chuckled and placed his hardening cock in my mouth. I forced it down my throat and swallowed over and over until it was in. Francisco gasped in surprise.

I held my breath and kept Cody buried down my throat for up to a minute at a time, with 10 or 20 seconds rest in my mouth. Over and over, I did this, allowing Cody to pump as hard as he pleased except during my little mouth breaks.

Francisco studied us like he was in school, taking notes. His notes were for nothing unless he had double-jointed jaw bones like mine.

Cody wanted to switch to regular sex in the butt, but I didn't want to give Francisco the pleasure of seeing it. We struggled a little before he won, and I obediently put my hands on the bathroom sink and presented my hole for him to use.

In this bathroom, there were lotions, cologne, and other expensive stuff that came with first class. Cody chose Rose Milk. The whole bathroom smelled of roses now. It wasn't perfect because it was designed to be absorbed by the skin. I slicked him up with some Tres Estrellas brilliantine, and the ride got smooth. The chemicals burned a little, but not as badly as Cody burned me when he used only lotion.

In three minutes, Cody was past the gates and inside my guts. Francisco rubbed himself in his pants. I loved the face of fear, jealousy, and awe that he wore. I wanted to punish him for taking my man. Cody would be mad if he knew what was going through my head. He would be even angrier if he knew what Francisco and I had just done in the office.

"Oh, God! Oh God! Cody, yes, yes." I said it not just because Cody was such an expert ass fucker, but because I knew it would mess with Francisco. Once you allow yourself to moan and shout with a dick like Cody's up your ass, there's no way to stop. "Jesus, please fuck me. Oh god, it feels so good. Fuck me. Fuck me, please, Daddy." I couldn't stop the words from pouring out of my mouth. Cody joined in.

"Yes, son. Yes, little son. You like it when Daddy fucks you with his big, fat cock, don't you?"

"Yes sir, oh yes sir. Please use my hole, Daddy." I didn't know why the words were so powerful, but they brought me to a climax quickly.

"Daddy, sir, I'm gonna make a puddle on your floor. I'm sorry, Daddy."

"Here, let Daddy help you." Cody put his hand under my cock and made a bowl to capture my cum. Like an obedient child, I shot my load into his hand.

I forgot Francisco was in the room. "You did not touch yourself?" He was astonished.

I rubbed it in, "When you can take a man like Cody this deep inside you, there ain't no need for sinning with your hands."

Cody sniffed my cum and tasted it. He furrowed his brow and frowned at me but drank it down. He made me lick myself clean. It tasted a little of cocaine. Oh no.

Cody must not have cared too much because he bucked and twisted, then I felt the familiar burst of cum fill my bottom. I made sure that Francisco saw it when Cody pulled out, and the soup of semen, hair oil, and lotion made a big puddle on the toilet floor.

The expression on Francisco's face was priceless. Like Texas, everything was bigger with Cody.

Back in the lounge, my dripping ass clean and dry, Cody mentioned the gift from Harry that had mysteriously disappeared.

I knew what was up. "I ain't gonna lie, Cody. Francisco knew what to do with it, so I went with him, and we did it."

"Did what?"

"Put it on each other's dicks and sniffed it up our noses."

Cody bellowed with laughter. "Brightie, you are too much!"

"What?"

"That part about your dicks, that's not normal."

"But it made sucking dick so much easier." I watched as Cody turned red and doubled over, gasping for air. I guess Francisco was not the expert he claimed to be.

❧ 30 ❧

SEGUROS

A pretty lady from Embraer entered the lounge and made an announcement.

"Regrettably, I must inform passengers to São Paulo that from conditions of weather, today's flight has been canceled."

I turned to Cody, who smiled and shrugged. "I guess we're gonna learn a little about Lima."

The taxi ride to the Gran Hotel Bolivar gave me a view of Lima and the coast. It went on forever. All the signs were in Spanish. I didn't know what the ads were for. Seguros appeared to be a local favorite. I asked the taxi driver what it meant.

"Insurance."

"Lima is huge. How many people live here?"

"Two million in the city. Many more just outside."

Two million! Dallas and Fort Worth combined are less than a million. Even Cody was impressed.

The hotel was a castle. Cody was my king, and I guess that made me his queen. A servant in uniform took the bags. They gave us a room with a balcony overlooking the central Plaza. The air smelled like oil wells and honeysuckle. Gold mirrors and candlesticks were hanging from the walls. Our beds were huge.

Cloth curtains hung down from a little shelf high above each bed.

We were both filthy, covered in different amounts of sweat, cum, lotion, airplane dust, and cocaine.

I wanted a bath, and Cody wanted a shower. From the tub, I watched him wash his big muscled body. As soap bubbled from deep within, his large hands got lost in the canyon between his butt cheeks. He used a lot of soap to wash the length of his fat, soft dick. He had soap on his face, so his eyes were closed. I loved watching him while he couldn't watch me back.

We put on clean jeans and cowboy shirts for dinner. The hotel was in the middle of everything, so Cody suggested we try some local food. We took a quiet street towards the park. Cody stopped and stared at a sign that said Baños Turcos. He smiled and grabbed my arm. All the men in Lima seemed comfortable walking arm in arm. I was nervous, but it didn't raise an eyebrow from the people rushing by. We found a little cafe with a Chinese waitress. Cody ordered for us.

The food that came was delicious, and it came with spicy sauce. Our plates had a pile of French Fries, some big chunks of onion and tomato fried up with thin beef strips. It was called 'saltado.'

TURKISH BATH

O n the way back to the hotel, Cody stopped at the Baños Turcos sign again. He smiled at me.

"Brightie, are you up for an adventure?"

"Everything that happened since we met has been an adventure. I ain't got no problem with it." Truth is, I would have followed Cody into hell if it meant I got to be with him.

"Let's go." He opened the door and invited me in. The first thing I noticed was the smell of cleaning supplies and mildew. There was a lady with a shawl taking coins from Cody. She handed us each a towel and a numbered key.

In the halls were a series of doors, some open, some closed. There were men in towels, men with towels over their shoulders, and men who must have lost their towels. In the rooms with open doors, there were all sorts of men. Short ugly ones, tall ugly ones, pretty boys, and muscled men. Some were lying face down, and some were lying on their backs. Some covered their heads with pillows like they were hiding. In the few rooms with closed doors, I could hear the sound of sex between men. Walking with Cody past these many rooms, we collected some admirers. They wore towels around their waists and followed us like dogs chasing a squirrel.

Cody unlocked his door and pulled me in, slamming it shut before the dogs could follow. He locked it.

I musta looked pretty confused.

"This is a Turkish Bath. There are showers, a big warm bath, a sauna, and a steam room. This is where married men go to have sex with queers."

"What?"

"You'll understand when you're older. What happens here is entirely up to you. We can shower and steam, we can have sex with or without each other, or we can turn around and go back to the hotel."

I was flustered. "I don't like sharing you with people."

Cody grinned. "There's more than enough for everyone." He grabbed his dick midway down his thigh.

I sighed inwardly, smiled, and said, "You know way more than I do. What would you like?"

Cody unbuttoned his shirt. "I would like people to watch us in envy like Harry or Francisco watched us. I want them to wish they had what we do."

That sounded good. I preferred to be with Cody.

We bought a small Vaseline at the front counter. Along the way, we picked up a bunch of admirers. Most of them saw Cody's swinging dick poking out from the hem of his towel. But some were watching me. We got a huge crowd to follow us into the steam room. We bared ourselves, but Cody used his body to say, "Look, but don't touch either of us." The steam made me pour out sweat.

Cody put a hand on my inner thigh and rubbed it gently. My cock was rock hard instantly. I grew faint from the heat. Cody licked my chest, spending time on each nipple. Then darkness.

I came to in his arms. He carried me to the bath. It was full of men, but there was room for two more. It was very warm, but not hot. An audience of men surrounded us, many of them tugging their penises from under their towels. All that attention made my dick hard. Some of the men were damned handsome. Cody took my hand. I followed him back to the room.

The crowd following us had grown to include most of the people in the building. They couldn't all fit in the room. Across from the room was a carpeted bench. Cody picked me up and placed me on my back. The crowd formed a circle around the bench. I rubbed Vaseline inside me and on Cody's pecker. He stroked to make it slippery. He spat. The crowd whispered and whistled as he grew hard. He was so huge soft; it was hard to believe he could grow so much more. I saw more than one man make the sign of the cross before returning to using their hands for sinful rubbing.

Cody put the head at my entryway. Heads were shaking. No one believed it was possible. I gave Cody a defiant nod. The crowd gave a loud gasp. He entered me in one smooth continuous motion, passing right through my butt and making a turn at the colon. His hips pressed hard against my bottom. I was stuffed to satisfaction. I was stretched and trembling from his giant cock.

The men watching us were all jerking themselves. They came at different times while Cody pumped his massive dick in and out of my stretched hole in a steady beat. I felt droplets of rain like before a storm comes.

More gasps when I trickled pre-cum and Cody sucked it from the end of my cock. Judging by some of the tiny penises around us, I knew those were gasps of envy and rage at God for cursing them.

Hands reached forward to touch my hard penis, but Cody, my big, strong protector, slapped them away. I opened my mouth to catch drops of sweat dripping from his forehead. I leaned forward and licked salty sweat from his abdomen. My tongue kept licking upwards until it found his nipples. I circled them several times before sucking on his teat. He threw his head back, eyes closed, and moaned. Several greedy paws took advantage of Cody's moment of blindness. Hands stroked every part of me that wasn't touching the bench or Cody. Like an angry bear, he opened his eyes and roared to scare off the crowd of gropers. It was a roar that meant, "He's my man, and you can't fuck him."

I doubled down on his left teat, the one above his heart. I clamped my mouth over it and began nursing like an infant. It was so good to have him in my mouth. I sucked as though he would give milk. I wrapped my legs around his waist, squeezing him with my thighs while he pistoned in and out of me.

Off to one side, I saw the next biggest dick in the place. I wanted it in my mouth. I gazed up at Cody. He read my mind.

I lay down with my head bent over the end of the bench. Cody sized up the very well-hung man, grunted, and snapped his fingers.

The great big dick rushed over. The head filled up my mouth until it pressed against my tonsils. I swallowed him like a hungry snake gobbling up a rat. The crown passed my airway and lodged itself deep in my throat. I didn't have to tell him; he knew when I needed air. He did a lot of deep fucking, and then he would spend a few seconds in my mouth, letting me breathe just long enough to take him deep again. He knew his dick well. I tasted salty pre-cum that had a flavor that was pure Cody. I glanced at my bull rider. He had enlisted a man with a tiny penis to play with his titties. The man was cross-eyed and missing some teeth. Cody had a good heart.

Cody saw me with my mouth full and read my mind again. I wanted to pass this well-hung man to Cody for some good ass-fucking.

Snap, snap. Now another handsome man had his penis in my mouth. Like every well-hung man, he liked to go deep, but he gave me a lot more time to breathe.

The big dicked man who had just choked me a dozen times was now rubbing Vaseline in my man's busy ass. Cody plowed in and out of me with long strokes. More pre-cum cascaded from my hard cock. Cody leaned in to lick it. This gave the big-dicked dude a chance to press his way in. With Cody's face so close to mine, I knew the moment he was penetrated. Then he made a soft whimper when his second sphincter was violated. He frowned when the man hit the back wall and smiled when he found the way beyond it.

My ass was stretched as far as I could stand, but as Cody's ass filled with big cock, his dick swelled up, opening my hole even further. I hadn't felt pain like this with Cody for a while. He was as hard as a man can get. He dribbled so much pre-cum that it acted like spit and made me slick inside. It relieved a lot of the pain this newer, bigger Cody was giving me.

The big dick was first. He bucked and pushed and relieved his hard dick inside Cody's asshole. The patient, handsome, well-hung man shot a quiet load in my mouth and pulled out. I wasn't used to taking a man's spew in my mouth. I looked up at Cody, who licked his lips, wanting my mouth full of semen. I shared it with him in a kiss so good that it put me over the edge. The first rope of my cum hit my forehead. Cody covered my cock and swallowed the rest. He licked my forehead to clean it. That brought several onlookers to shoot at the same time. The sprinkles became showers. In less than a minute, we were soaking wet with Peruvian semen. Every square inch of exposed flesh was covered in the male milk. Most landed on Cody's broad back, which covered me now as he returned to deep eight-inch strokes.

My ass quivered. It was so stretched and satisfied, my ass couldn't stop the spasms. Squeezing Cody's nipples brought the sex to its natural end. With snorts and grunts, Cody whipped in and out in a blur, causing me to have an internal orgasm. I moaned and bucked as my insides spasmed more and more. They were Cody's undoing. He fired load after hot load into my butt. The contractions caused some juice to fire out around Cody and hit bystanders. Another rain shower of come landed on us. Cody looked like he had walked through a tube of Brylcreem. I must have too.

My worn-out ass pushed out Cody's dick, which hit his thigh with a loud clap. We staggered to the showers, washing the juice of a hundred lost babies from our bodies. The showers were full of men waiting for an encore. Cody smiled and shrugged. It sent them all away. In the shower together, we kissed until the water turned cold. We steamed to open our pores, then showered in cold water to close them. It was my first time in a Turkish bath; it wouldn't be the last.

❧ 32 ❧

HIGH AGAIN

Leaving the bath, we ran smack into Harry, the cocaine salesman. He hugged us both and thanked us for the best fuck of his life.

"Oh, you two, everything pales in comparison. Did you like my gift, Brightie?"

I had to be careful. Cody wasn't exactly pleased with Harry for giving me drugs.

"It was really somethin' different." I learned to use that phrase with my mom's cooking until she caught on.

"Great. It's a brand-new business. I'm bringing it to Texas and California. I think it will be a hit!"

"But Harry," I asked, "Isn't it illegal?"

"It is, but the FBN are the enforcers. They're on their last legs. I'm sure we'll have cocaine on supermarket shelves in the next few years."

"What about here in Peru?"

"Here, they don't have enough money to hire someone to arrest me. The jurisdiction is supposed to be shared between the Guardia Civil and the Peruvian Investigative Police. Neither agency is funded properly, so each one gives responsibility for enforcement to the other. It's perfect. Nobody has ever been arrested for exporting cocaine. It just isn't financially possible, which creates a giant loophole."

"What's the punishment if you were caught?"

"Death."

Harry hugged Cody and rubbed his bottom. "Such a big man! Mmm!"

As he hugged me, he dropped a wax envelope into my shirt pocket. He whispered, "Another sample since you liked it so much."

Back at the hotel, I had to decide what to do. If the weather cooperated, we were leaving in the morning for Brazil. If I brought cocaine into Brazil, it would be a much more dangerous crime. Cody mentioned they search for cocaine on any flights from Peru. They would just make you disappear forever if you were caught. Harry was an asshole. I confessed to Cody.

"Why did you take it?"

"I was hugging him; he took advantage. I told you as soon as I could."

Cody nodded.

"I'm going to flush it down the toilet." I walked towards the bathroom.

"No, wait!" Cody surprised me. "Let's not waste it."

Cody was intrigued by my adventure with Francisco.

"I can't get the picture out of my mind, Brightie. Snorting coke off your dick. Fuck it; we only live once."

My dick went hard right away. Cody took longer because of all the blood needed to make him hard. Watching his cock go from a soft giant to a hard monster was exciting. Once we both stood at attention, Cody covered my cock in coke. He tapped the white powder on his enormous log of meat. Too much surface; we were gonna run out. He didn't put a lot, or so it seemed.

I went first, inhaling the tingly powder and flying around the chandelier. The unnatural size of Cody's hard dick fooled the eye. That was a ton of cocaine.

Cody made me jump when he held my dick like a fat cigar. His hands were so big and gentle. When his nose slid down my dick, snorting along my flesh, I let out a surprise dribble of pre-come. His mustache tickled. The high lasted about ten minutes, and then we landed hard. We went back for more. This envelope was a lot larger than the little bag Harry had given me before.

I don't remember when sniffing became sucking. We sixty-nined, sucking each other for a long time with our throats so numb. Cody held my ass and pushed me deeper down his throat. He was deep in my throat, but it wasn't the whole way. I grabbed hold of his two big flesh mountains and forced him in all the way to the base. With all the cocaine buzzing through my head, I convinced myself that I was a baby bird and Cody's giant worm would feed me when it exploded. I was so hungry. I needed Cody to feed me. It was an obsession. I nearly passed out when I didn't come up for air.

There was more cocaine, more holding each other in our mouths, and more hands pressing and pulling on asses to feed the baby birds. Time became a blur. I was still waiting for my meal. I wouldn't feed Cody until he fed me. We stayed locked in our sniffing-sucking loop until I tasted the first sweet drop of pre-come on the tip of Cody's dick. As usual, this caused me to follow; I leaked the sticky clear stuff into Cody's throat. This excited him, and he gave me a real gusher of the stuff. That excited me so much; I couldn't wait any longer.

I bucked, shook, and shot my sperm in Cody's mouth when he pulled back for air. I pressed my face until Cody's massive balls smacked my chin, ensuring he was as deep in my throat as he could be. My gusher was the trigger. Cody moaned and thrashed, but I wouldn't let him out. My cheeks and nose were buried in his big balls when they came together and pulled up tight. I heard and felt the come being forced out of him as it made the very long journey up his shaft to my throat. He gained momentum in his hips, and the combined action shot his white hot sperm real hard. It was like someone turned on a garden hose near my voice box, and my whole throat was coated in hungry bird dinner. When we were drained, we unlocked from one another. The faint light of dawn lighted the room, and the cocaine was all gone. Mission accomplished.

🦋 33 🦋

SOUTH AMERICAN WAY

The flight to Sao Paulo was horrible. Our plane was bigger, but it had to climb several miles to make it over the Andes. Then when we reached the hot air of the Amazon basin, the plane hit what the captain called "turbulence." We had to stay belted in our seats for two hours while the plane jumped and thrashed like a fish in a dry bucket. I had a hangover from last night's sex and a sore throat from sucking Cody all night. My throat muscles ached; I could only speak in a whisper. And my jaw muscles kept cramping. Cody didn't fare much better. Even the stewardesses had to stay strapped in for safety, so they didn't serve us food. It was only when we reached the Atlantic coast that the plane stopped jumping and bumping. We were beginning our descent into Sao Paulo, and there was no time to serve us our meal.

Stepping off the plane, I expected Sao Paulo to be hot and sticky, like Houston. It was cool and mild. Cody reminded me that it was Autumn in the Southern Hemisphere.

Sao Paulo was the biggest city I had ever seen. There were no houses; everyone lived in a giant sea of new apartments. The apartments were not skyscrapers, but they were taller than anything in Clinton. Most of them looked to be ten stories high. And they were all around the airport, stretching for miles in every direction. You could fit Dallas in here ten times or more.

"Cody, how many people live here?"

"I don't know exactly, but it's between 4 and 5 million."

That was bigger than Chicago. It was huge.

We hired a limousine to take us to Barretos, where the festival was. The driver spoke enough English to understand our destination, but not a word more.

He kept pronouncing it ba-HAY-twos. It was spelled Barretos. I hoped he had the right town.

He managed to explain that it was a six-hour drive. Luckily, I grew up in Oklahoma, where most places are six hours away. I could take a trip like that in the back of a pickup truck. A limousine was going to be easy.

As we passed through the inner city streets, I saw men on bicycles with giant yellow and green fruit. They carried it over their shoulders, hanging from a long branch.

Cody said, "Sugar Apples."

"What?"

"Sugar Apples, that's what they call them in Texas. In Brazil, they must be something else."

"Fruit-uh gee congee." At least, that's what it sounded like the driver said. Congee.

After an hour of driving through city streets, we reached the outskirts of Sao Paulo. Naked children were playing in the mud. I thought it was cute until I realized the mud was sewer water. There were so many of them. Above them was a hillside covered in cement shacks. As crowds formed, the driver did just the opposite of what we would do if people were crossing the street in Oklahoma. He sped up, so everyone had to either jump out of our way or get run over.

He shook his head and said, "Favelas."

Cody nudged me. "Slums."

"Yeah, I kinda figured. But why did he try to run them down? Isn't it hard enough being poor?"

Cody smiled. "You make a good point. But it was for survival. He didn't want to kill anyone, but many of them would kill us for our money. So he used the car to drive them back."

As if to prove Cody's point, I heard a gun go off. It didn't hit our car, but it could have.

Once we left the city, everything was a greener version of Oklahoma. I saw farms, cows, chickens, corn, beans, horses, farmers, pigs - everything looked like a farm at home except different. Some of the farmhouses were made out of mud or recycled wood. A few were made from beautiful dark wood with carved balconies and a stone chimney. Some were like the farms in Texas, with tile roofs and white adobe walls. The cows were not like our cows. They were white and tall. The pigs were black instead of pink. Still, it was more like home than anywhere else I had been in South America. I laid back and smiled

❧ 34 ❧
POTHOLES

C ody asked the driver to roll up the window between him and us. He closed the curtains, so we were suddenly in a private room in the back of a car.

Cody pulled me to him and kissed me hard. "I want you, Brightie." He rubbed his pants leg, staring at me like a hungry lion at a piece of steak.

I put my hand on his long, thick penis growing under the pant legs.

"We better get your pants off before you're trapped."

Cody pulled off his cowboy boots, unbuckled, and gave me the cuffs of his jeans.

"It's already too late, you sexy clown. You gotta pull these off me."

Cody was rock hard, and his big meaty left thigh was trapped. I pulled, and Cody pushed until the jeans budged. They got stuck again, so I put my foot on Cody's armpit for leverage and pulled hard. The jeans flew off, leaving Cody naked, rock-hard, and horny.

Cody had Albolene in his backpack. He applied it to my asshole, worked it in with his finger, then coated his massive hard-on with the slippery lotion.

I raised my knees to my ears, giving Cody a clear

path. I was so used to him now that it didn't hurt when he passed through the two rings, rounded the corner, and filled my belly with his giant cock. It was heaven. Every inch of my insides was wrapped tight around Cody's big cock. The tight fit made us both feel good because his skin touched me as he moved in and out.

I couldn't help myself; I moaned like a woman.

Cody covered my mouth with his as if to swallow my moans of pleasure. Cody was very gentle. I wanted it rough.

"Fuck me harder, Daddy."

He needed no further encouragement. In a flash, the sex switched from slow and sensual to rough and brutal. I was grateful that Cody had loosened me up so much. This was the roughest he'd ever been. It hurt, but it was a good kind of hurt; it made me glad to be alive.

I couldn't believe I heard myself say, "Harder!"

Now Cody was punching my gut with the massive head of his cock. My butthole was stretching as the excitement of rough sex made Cody harder. The limousine was going fast when we hit a pothole. The car bounced at the same time that Cody punched his way deep into my guts. It felt wrong; the pain was blinding. But then it disappeared, and we went back to the crazy hard fucking. The pain was pleasure now. Cody became an animal, fucking fast and hard to leave his semen inside me. My legs were wrapped around his waist. There was nowhere to be except under this big brute who fucked me silly. His sweat landed on my tongue until he shook his head with passion, showering me with it. The smell drove me wild. I bucked to meet his thrusts. He pummeled my insides. That sweaty musk caused me to have a surprise orgasm. I squirted in the narrow space between our bellies and chests. I wasn't touching myself.

Cody smiled at me with astonishment. "Did you just come?"

I nodded.

"How do you do that?"

"I don't; you do it to me."

That compliment landed hard. In moments, he was breathing heavy. He made a snail trail of pre-cum up inside me. He was close.

"Oh God, Brightie! What did I do to deserve you?"

His thrusting turned painful again now that I was done coming. I took the shortcut; I pinched Cody's nipples.

"Aaaaahrghh!" It was like I had pressed the orgasm button. Then came a hot gush in my guts as Cody pushed hard, deeper than he had ever been, and lay his forehead on my chest. It sounded like he was crying.

"You okay, Daddy?" I kissed the crown of his soaking wet head, tasting his smell.

Cody locked eyes with me, tears streaming down his cheeks. "It's like I told you, Brightie. Until I met you, no one could take me. I gave up all hope of ever having sex the way I wanted."

"Any time you want."

He wiped the tears away and kissed me. His mustache was wet from his tears.

Cody was stuck deep in my colon so I couldn't push him out. He pulled his cock from me hand over hand like lifting a bucket out of a well until he popped loose and semen gushed on the limousine floor.

Cody mixed us drinks while I grabbed a towel and cleaned up my gravy spill. It was not just semen; there was blood. I hid the towel from Cody at the bottom of the wastebasket.

We drank bourbon and ginger ale, then slept until we reached Barretos in the late afternoon.

35

A BED IN BARRETOS

I was under the weather when we got to our modern hotel in Barretos. The town was dressed up in Rodeo banners and Brazilian flags. I couldn't read any of it but the dates: Friday, Saturday, and Sunday. They called the days of the week by numbers. Cody said we needed to find something to eat, but I didn't want to right then. My belly ached and was a little swollen. I thought maybe it was some bad water. But when I went to the toilet, all blood came out. It scared me so bad I made a noise, and Cody came rushing in. He put his hand on my forehead.

"You're running a fever."

"I feel cold. How can I have a fever?"

"Brightie, can you pull up your pants? I need to take you to the doctor."

Lucky it was a Thursday because the medical clinic was open. Everything closes down starting Friday for Rodeo. Cody wrapped me in a blanket to stop my shivering and carried me downstairs like a bridesmaid. I saw little spots in front of my eyes when we stepped outside. I thought maybe this is what dying is like. It wasn't too bad. I leaned my head back and closed my eyes.

"Stay with me, Brightie!" Cody shook me hard. I

covered his neck with my arms and put my nose in the hollow above the collarbone. A taxi was waiting in front of the hotel.

Cody must know enough Spanish to fool the Brazilians into understanding him.

The last thing I heard him say was, "Santa Maria."

When I came to, it was dark outside. A nurse gave me an injection of something that turned the whole world nice.

"What is that?" I asked her. She shook her head. "No English."

Cody leaped out of the chair. He came over to my bed. His face was twisted with worry.

"It's okay; I'm alive."

Cody had tears in his eyes. "Thank God. I am so sorry."

I was confused.

"I drank some swamp water or something. It ain't your fault! How could it be your fault?"

Cody held his cowboy hat between his hands and didn't say anything.

"The doctor will tell you, so I'd rather you hear it from me. Brightie, I think I ripped you open back on that bumpy road."

I thought back to that moment when it felt real wrong. Yeah, I guess maybe he did.

"It was an accident."

"I almost killed you!" Cody wiped tears away.

"So did every bull I ever fought, and you ever rode. But we're both alive."

Cody's hangdog face made me so sad. I could never understand what it must be like to be so abnormal. I am lucky I never have to worry about that stuff. Hell, before he met me, he was sort of a virgin, I think.

Since nobody spoke English nearby, I thought I should have a frank discussion.

"Cody, you said I was the first."

"I said you were the first who could take me."

"So, has this happened before?"

Cody didn't answer. The shame broke my heart. He just nodded.

I was all warm and fuzzy from whatever that nurse gave me.

"How bad was it? It's not like anybody died, right?"

Cody lashed out. Not at me. At the world. "I never asked for this!" He grabbed the monster in his pant leg. "It's not fair. Brightie, you were so perfect. I thought, at last, I had found the one person in the world meant just for me."

"You did, Cody. Me."

He pointed to my hospital bed. "No, I didn't. It happened to you, too."

"It happened on a road filled with potholes." I couldn't believe I had to explain it to him like a child. I guess this was a real sore subject for him.

"It could happen again anywhere."

"I doubt it. I remember the exact moment it happened. In the past, you didn't even come close. It was just one of those moments."

"How many more will there be?"

"I don't know, and I don't care, so long as I'm spending those moments with you."

I saw a spark, a little flame that had gone out. It came back to life. Cody was still tore up with guilt, but he was not going to give up on me.

I kept the little spark going until it could burn like a flame. "Let me ask you, how many of the people you injured were bull-riders? Or bullfighters like me?"

"None of them."

"See, we're cut from a different cloth, you and me. We get thrown off the bull, but we climb right back on, right?"

I could tell now that Cody wanted to kiss me, but we were in a room with two nurses, another patient, and the patient's family. I blew him an air kiss right before the fuzziness took over and the darkness descended.

ILLEGALLY LARGE

When I woke again, Cody was gone. A doctor was sitting by my bed, taking notes. He smiled and picked up a clipboard. He read through it before speaking to me in pretty good English.

"Young man, your name is Brighton?"

"Yes, but I go by Brightie."

"Brightie. Okay. He made a note on his clipboard."

"Where's Cody?"

"Your friend? He must stay in the waiting room. He is not family."

"He's my uncle."

"I hope that is not true."

I thought about what he meant by that. It made me mad, but I didn't want to fight.

"So when can I leave?"

"You were fortunate. The tear in your colon was superficial. You lost much blood, but it is healing already."

I nodded.

"The thing is, I must ask you, how did this tear happen?"

I didn't want to answer this. I was in Brazil. Who knows what a truthful answer would bring?

"I, uh, I'm not sure. What could cause it?"

The doctor sighed.

"If it were in the rectum, I would say that passive anal sex was the cause. But this was here, deep in your colon." He pointed to a chart that gave me all kinds of names and information about the inside of a man's butt.

I didn't know how to react, but I needed to real quick.

"I thought it was a bug in the water. I didn't have no anal sex. '

"A superficial examination indicated otherwise. You are a catamite."

"A cata-what?"

"I will not waste time with this. You know this is true. What I need to know is if your friend out there should be arrested."

"No, why?"

"We believe he has engaged in, eh, forbidden sexual practices."

"I didn't know there was laws about that kind of stuff."

"See, that's better; you are not wasting my time denying."

"So sex between men is illegal?"

"No, actually, between two grown men in Brazil, it is legal. You are an adult."

"I don't understand."

"My son, the only way you could have been injured in that manner would be if he used his eh hands in you. That is the only way he could reach so far. This is an illegal lewd act, and I must report it."

"I'm afraid you're mistaken, sir."

The doctor pushed his glasses toward his forehead. "I cannot be. This is the only way you could have received your injury."

"Call my friend in here. I want him to explain."

"This is highly irregular, but yes."

A minute later, Cody walked into the room. The doctor frowned. "What is it you wish to show me."

"Cody, they're gonna arrest you for improper sexual practices unless you show him your dick."

Cody wore a snarl. He turned with his back to the family across the way, so only me and the doctor could see. Cody took his time, pulling his dick out of the top of his jeans. The doctor's eyes grew wider and wider with each inch Cody revealed. It doubled over on itself as he hauled it out of his pant leg. At last, it flopped out the top and cascaded down to his knees.

The doctor made the sign of the cross. Just to torment him a little further, Cody turned himself on until it swelled and began to rise.

The doctor mopped his brow with a white handkerchief. He was pale.

"This will continue to happen, as it must have happened many times."

I laughed. "This was the first, an accident that won't ever repeat." Cody nodded in agreement.

"Doc, how soon can I get back to being a catamite?"

Cody and the doctor burst out laughing. The doctor answered. Saturday was the soonest I could return to having sex in the butt. It was going to be torture.

I studied that diagram of the bowels while we waited for the paperwork to arrive. For me to see Cody poke out my belly, he had to go far. I was shocked how deep in my sigmoid colon Cody musta gone.

CRUELTY

The doctor released me in time for us to catch a late dinner at a Steakhouse. It was all you could eat. I never ate so much meat in all my life. Brahma, the only beer on the menu, tasted a lot like Budweiser.

We staggered back to the hotel, both a little tipsy. I was still recovering from the fuzzy medicine the nurse gave me.

Cody flopped face down on the bed and unbuckled his jeans. They didn't fall to the floor because they were hung up on his big ole cock again. He could only push the jeans down to somewhere above his knees. I saw his muscular, shiny ass in the moonlight.

"It's your turn, Brightie."

Gazing at the twin mountains of his butt, my pecker got rock hard. I buried my nose in that canyon and tongued his butthole. He wiggled so hard, he smacked my nose with his rock-hard butt cheeks.

"Brightie, I got so scared. I can't lose you."

I came up for air. "I ain't a porcelain clown you can lose; I'm a rodeo clown. I won't let go."

Cody grew quiet as I put my tongue deeper and deeper into his anus. I was getting good at it. He moaned. I let spit build up in my mouth, hocked a loogie, then pushed it all inside Cody with my tongue. My dick was hard. I put my middle finger in Cody's butt. He squirmed and growled. He handed me a tub of Albolene, which I smeared inside Cody's poop chute. I took a second helping of the white grease and coated my dick until it shined. I let one, two, three wads of spit fall from my mouth onto my dick. Cody was wriggling like a nightcrawler. I pushed his waist into the bed and poked my thick dick through his slippery hole. He was so calm as I passed the second sphincter. He didn't flinch when I bumped hard into the back wall of the rectum. He squealed like a pig when I turned him just right so as I could turn the corner and put the whole head into his sigmoid colon. I was so close. I pushed, spreading Cody's buttocks apart to go deeper. At last, the crown popped past the bend, and I was in. Cody turned back to smile at me.

"Brightie, you're doing great for someone so new to this."

I flushed at the backhanded compliment.

"I could say the same for you. One injury, zero deaths." I laughed at my joke, but Cody froze. He was still and silent for a whole minute while I rode him. Then he pushed back hard right when I pounded my way in. He knocked me off balance. It was angry sex. Cody humped back on me hard, and I just had to stand there or else topple over if I tried to move. It was not the friendly sex we had before. It was Cody using my dick like it was a toy. He didn't say nothing, but he grunted.

"Cody, what's happening?"

"Just shut up and stand still." He continued to ride up and down my dick. There was no mutual pleasure. He was like a mechanical milking machine.

"Did I say something wrong?"

"I told you to shut your mouth."

I wanted to cry. This was not the sex we had before

the accident in the limousine. He wanted complete control of everything that was happening. He rotated so he was on his back, his jeans bunched up at his knees. He put the stuck jeans around my neck.

"I can't get my fucking pants off, Brightie. I have a monster; what am I supposed to do?"

He pounded himself with my dick. It was like I wasn't even there. He rubbed up and down his leg until a wet stain of pre-come showed.

"You are so fucking lucky you have a normal dick."

I began, "Yours is so huge, I love—" He cut me off.

"I told you to keep quiet. Now, hurry up." Cody grabbed my nipples and twisted them painfully. It still worked. I released a small helping of pre-come in Cody's ass. It made everything twice as slippery. Cody was still using my dick like it was his property. He was rubbing himself hard. I wanted to be in step with him like we always was before. But we just became two strangers using each other.

I shot my wad first. It happened during one of Cody's upstrokes, so I wasn't all the way in. Sad and blue, I filled his rectum half-heartedly with my cum. He didn't even notice until it leaked on the bedspread.

"Did you shoot your load before me?"

"Well, yeah, Cody."

"Shut up!" He had no hope of freeing his giant cock from his jeans, so he rubbed real hard along the part he had managed to expose.

"Pinch my fucking nipples!" I didn't like him cursing at me, but I did what he asked.

"Oh, oh yeah." Cody's smile of pleasure was the only nice thing I'd seen for the past twenty minutes. He yanked up and down real hard like he was putting rosin on a strap.

"Oh fuck!" Again with the curse words. "Oh shit! Fuck me, you fucking piece of shit!" Words can't describe how bad he made me feel right then. But I wanted to make him happy, so I pulled and pushed my soft dick in and out as best I could.

"Mmm. Yeah, boy!" Cody took care of himself, "Oh shit, this is it!" I leaned forward to kiss him, but he pushed me away.

"I'm there. Pinch harder!"

Cody roughly grabbed my hands and used his thumb and index finger to force my fingers to pinch his nipples. He let go when I could clamp down hard enough to please him.

With no sound, he came. I knew because of the growing wet stain on his jeans. He pulled away from me. I flopped out of him, still shiny with Albolene.

Cody came out of the bathroom five minutes later. He was out of his jeans. I tossed him his flannel pajamas. He threw them right back at me. In twenty minutes, he was snoring.

❧ 38 ❧

GUILHERME

In the morning, we searched the town for a real breakfast. Our hotel had coffee, bread, fruit, and square donuts without holes. We wanted meat and eggs. We found a cafeteria that had ham and grits; it was close enough. The grits were big and yellow, and they called them kooshkoosh.

After a nap, we got ready for the Friday evening rodeo. We weren't official contestants; we were part of an exhibition event on Saturday night. We would demonstrate the American rodeo. Mexico was gonna do something called "charreada." So we got to sit out Friday and watch the Brazilian cowboys (or peaõs) compete against each other at the Recinto Paulo de Lima Correia.

I am no expert at counting. I can say that the Brazil rodeo in Barretos was more than five times as big as any rodeo I'd ever worked in the US. I was amazed that here, in a place so far away that the seasons weren't even the same, the rodeo was such a big deal. Friday was trick riding and horse tripping. It's all the stuff we leave out of the rodeo back home. The bulls were on display in a tent in wooden pens that gave them enough room to run and crack the fence. The kids were too close. It wasn't my business, so I ignored it. Nobody was getting hurt.

Guilherme, the manager of the rodeo, approached Cody and me. He stared at my blond hair and blue eyes. Cody shook his hand and introduced me. The whole time, the guy was checking Cody out below the waist. I would have been pissed about it, but he was also checking me out, front and back like I was some prize bull he bought at the county fair. In a way, I guess we were.

Guilherme was movie-star handsome. He had big full lips, light brown skin, green eyes, black jeans, and a black cowboy shirt, and he topped it off with a white cowboy hat. Guilherme's cowboy boots, made from black alligator, were clean and perfect like he spent a lot of time cleaning them.

Cody embraced Guilherme at the shoulders and said something in Portuguese that I couldn't understand. Guilherme put his arms around Cody's waist. All the while, he watched me like a weasel watching the henhouse. After a few minutes, he let Cody go and scampered off to deal with some rodeo problem.

"What was that about?" I asked Cody, the anger returning.

"Relax, Brightie. He's the one writing the checks. He's one of us. A little hug was my way of thanking him for sweetening the pot."

"What do you mean?"

Cody cleared his throat. "Brightie, do you see that crowd? It's twelve thousand people. Most of them paid a few dollars to get in. Some paid a lot more. They're coming back tomorrow, and Sunday, too. I told Guilherme we were a good pair, and he should pay us better, seeing's how you ended up in the hospital and all."

I turned bright red; my ears gave off heat. "They didn't charge me none, so I don't see why you were telling him our private business."

"Oh, believe me," Cody chuckled, "our business is not private. That doctor told him everything."

"What!?" I was embarrassed, angry, upset, and a hundred other things all at once. "That goddamned doctor! He thought you put your arm in me."

Cody scanned the crowd cautiously. "Hey Brightie, it's rare for someone here to speak English, but it only takes one."

Cody was right, and I was still pissed off. "So you never finished about the sweet pot."

"Oh, yeah. Because of the turnout, I asked for a thousand dollars each."

My jaw dropped.

"Cody, that's more money than I've made in all my days as a clown."

"Welcome to the big time, kid." He cleared his throat. I sensed there was something more.

"Do we have to do anything extra to earn it?"

"Not in the arena."

I smelled a rat. "What do we have to do with Guilherme, then?"

Cody screwed his face up into a cold sneer. He put his finger on my chest. "You're mine, do you understand? What I say goes. You will go where I want when I want, and I don't want any complaints."

I wanted to say it scared me like I was sold into slavery with no way out. But it wasn't fear. I was aroused. My dick went hard in my jeans.

"Y-yes, sir. Sorry, sir." I hung my head. I wanted to rebel, to fight back against Cody's control, but my spirit felt better when I submitted to him.

"Good. Now, I promised you to Guilherme. He's got a great big dick, huge. But he's not as big as me. Hope you can handle that."

This was a different Cody. I missed the man who cried when I took all of him inside me. This Cody was a tyrant. But damn if I didn't obey.

"Yes, sir. Whatever you want, sir." Cody liked that. I saw him grow big and hard in his jeans. I knew I had a tiny bit of power over him when I saw that. Like he can't control everything. It was a crumb, a scrap of dignity I held on to.

The men in Brazil were different from back home. The cowboys were all the colors of the rainbow. We have one or two black bull riders, but in Brazil, they were everywhere. Many guys were white, but like Guilherme, they had black hair and brown skin. Then there were pale blonde guys whiter than me.

"Cody, why are there so many black people in Brazil?"

Cody smiled. "It's a long story. There was slavery here, a lot like in the US."

I pointed to a guy who was light brown but had curly hair. "Like him; how did he get that color?"

"He's probably a Pardo. That's a man who's mostly European, like Portuguese or Italian, but he has some African in him, too."

Back home, if a white and a black got together, it was illegal in a lot of places. Here in Brazil, it was different. Men could be with men, blacks, and whites...this was a free country. Freer than ours.

"Is Guilherme black?"

"No. Black is black. He's pardo. He's got black in him. Some Indian too."

"Like Cherokee Indian?"

Cody shook his head. "They got different tribes down here, but yeah, sort of."

For the time being, he'd stopped being the master, and I wasn't the servant. I guess it would just happen whenever he felt like it.

Working in the rodeo, you don't get as excited as the crowd. I watched a bronco rider; it looked just like back home. The only difference was the shouts were in another language, and the weather was better. The beer was cheap and delicious. It was called Paulista. I got a little carried away, and as midnight drew near, I felt my-self floating out of my boots.

❧ 39 ❧

WHORED OUT

When the Friday exhibition ended, Guilherme was right by my side. He took my arm and smiled. I wanted to pull it away, but Cody was back to being the master. He stared at me hard. I swallowed.

"Oh, you beautiful boy. You are so sweet." Guilherme was pretty good with English. "I hope Cody has informed you what will be happening now."

Cody jumped in. "He knows."

I didn't know, but I guessed what it was.

Guilherme drove an American Chevrolet pickup truck. Cody waited for me to climb up, then sat pressed close to me. I was the bologna in a man sandwich.

Guilherme lived on a ranch way out of town. The bumpy road reminded me of what happened on Thursday. The doctor told me to wait until Saturday. But it was after midnight, so it was Saturday. I wanted to talk to Guilherme and learn more about him, but every time I opened my drunk mouth, Cody clenched my arm between his huge thumb and forefinger. The trip wasn't long in hours or miles but it felt like an eternity. I felt like puking, but it passed. My drunken happiness wore off.

Guilherme's truck had shock absorbers, but they

didn't help smooth the pitted dirt road with no street lights. Moths flew in front of the car headlights and covered the window in butterfly blood. Why did I feel like a butterfly in the collector's jar? We came close to smacking into the side of a big white cow. Guilherme cursed. I didn't know the words, but you just know when it's cursing.

Cody put his arm up on the back of the truck seat and let his big hands dangle down to touch my neck. I felt chills of excitement and also anger. I don't know much about prostitutes, but I think that's what we were doing. I seen lady prostitutes at the rodeo. We called them bull flies. They wore pretty skirts and blouses, but their hair wasn't washed. They had tears in their nylons too. I considered my outfit. Thanks to Cody, I had on tight jeans, a cowboy shirt that was so tight you could see my nipples, and a baby blue kerchief tied to my neck. Is this what a man whore dresses like? I was about to find out.

❧ 40 ❧

HOW A WHORE EARNS
HIS PAY

Guilherme turned off the dirt road onto a paved driveway. Weird how the road has no paving, but the house does. Guilherme's house was something out of a magazine. The roof seemed to be floating because there was so much glass at the top. His swimming pool light was on, and it lit up the floating white roof with the reflected ripples. At night, his garden was just the outlines of something dark, impossible to see. When he entered the front door, he switched on the light and turned on the garden lights. I caught my breath before it escaped. He had flowers like nothing I'd ever seen before. Big bushes, long trailing vines, fruit trees, flowers, prairie grass, and stone benches for sitting and admiring the plants.

Inside, the house expanded in every direction.

"Do you like my house, Brightie?"

I nodded.

"It's an Oscar Niemeyer. He is a famous architect here, but maybe you don't know him. He built hundreds of buildings in our capital. Very talented man."

Guilherme made us a drink called Caipirinha. The liquor was like rum but not as sweet, so the lime and the sugar made it all balance and tasted like you were drinking lemonade. That was a problem, actually. I was

so nervous about my upcoming thousand-dollar performance I gulped instead of sipping. My first drink was
replaced with another. By the time I finished it, I was
happy from drinking, like I felt at the steakhouse after
a bunch of beers.

Guilherme stood and gestured toward the center of
the house.

"I gave my staff the night off, and we must make do
ourselves."

I asked Cody if he ever gave his staff time off, and
he put a finger to his lips. Guilherme wasn't within
hearing distance, so Cody leaned down and whispered,
"Don't talk more than you have to. I don't want him to
know I have a big house. We're cowboys, remember."

I nodded. It made sense. Cody wasn't mean or mad;
he just wanted me to act right in front of Guilherme.

A long walk down a glass corridor brought us to a
bedroom. The round bed was covered with a pink bedspread and six giant pillows. The ceiling above the bed
had a mirror. There were a lot of mirrors in the room.
Guilherme went into a closet bigger than my bedroom
and came out in a bathrobe.

"Do you gentlemen want to get more comfortable?
Perhaps take off your things." It began as a question but
ended up more like a command. Cody sat on the edge
of the bed to remove his boots. I sat near him. I unbuttoned my jeans, but Guilherme interrupted.

"No, son. Those are later. Start with your shirt."
Cody had already taken his off and stood so our host
could admire the prize bull for sale.

He pointed to the place where Cody's balls lived.

"This does not match your reputation. I expected
more." Cody grinned.

"Here." He took the Brazilian's hand and put it
midway on his thigh. "That's the middle."

Guilherme was ready to faint. "And you fuck men
with that?"

Cody pushed his hand further until they were almost at the knee. That's where it ended when it was soft. I already knew this. I didn't want Guilherme to know, but I wanted a thousand dollars, so I kept my mouth shut.

"But this is not even hard? Does it grow bigger?"

Cody nodded. "Mostly girth, not so much lengthwise."

He was being modest. He grew a lot in every direction. That's why he has to take his jeans off before he gets hard.

Guilherme was a very handsome man. If he and Cody did too much, he'd wind up trapped in those jeans. They weren't tight, but Cody's cock was too much for the loosest pants.

Guilherme smiled at me and came over to appraise me. He put his hands on my arms, my chest, my butt - I half expected him to check my mouth for fillings. He found his way down to my jeans and nodded approval. After Cody, what could I offer?

"Yours is very nice. I will enjoy holding it while I fuck you."

I glanced over at Cody for support. He checked his watch and shrugged.

Guilherme didn't hesitate. He was nosy. "Are you and Cody, um together?" Cody gazed at his nails and shook his head. That shouldn't hurt, but it did.

"No. We're good friends."

Cody took one hand and drew it across his neck like a knife. He wanted me to stay quiet. It was subtle; I nearly missed it.

"What kind of friends?"

I know Cody told me not to talk, but this was tricky. If I hesitated, he would know I was lying. So in that split second, I said the perfect thing.

"I'm his clown. I've saved his butt a bunch of times."

Guilherme grinned. "Shame, really. It seems like you two could be so much more than just friends. Please excuse me for a moment. He ducked into a bathroom and closed the door.

Cody came close to me, "Good save, Brightie."

"What are we supposed to be?"

"Just two cowboys who like to play with the big boss."

Having to pretend not to love Cody was hard work. I was earning my money.

When Guilherme came back into the bedroom, he motioned for Cody to go. In a few minutes, Cody came out with a wet spot on the butt of his jeans.

"Now, it is your turn."

Cody could see I didn't know what he wanted me to do. "Come on; it's fun. I'll show you."

Cody brought me into the bathroom and yanked down my pants. He made me sit on a urinal, but it wasn't like any I ever seen. It had hot and cold taps and made a fountain of water. Cody sat me on it and turned up the water. I tried to jump, but he kept his hand on me.

"Relax, let it all go."

And I did. The water went right up inside me, and when it came out, it had changed color. It was a familiar feeling, but not as uncomfortable as the enema that Cody gave me back in Texas. It didn't take long before the water was clear.

"Good. No blood." Cody was all business.

"Cody, you aren't doing this for the money. Why are you doing it?"

"It's good for both of our careers. We'll be here every year, and pretty soon, we'll compete."

"But it's Brazil. The money can't be that much."

Come on; he guided me by the neck out of the room and into an open bathrobe full of Guilherme.

"You may remove those now." I shucked off my

jeans and put them near my other things. I didn't have no underwear. Guilherme held another Caipirinha in his hand, giving it to me while he danced to invisible music.

I did a double-take when I saw what he had between his legs. It was enormous, hanging down like a dark cobra.

"I am bigger than you," he said, teasing me, "You know what that means."

I didn't, but I played along. I don't know if it was Brazilians or just him, but he did things in a funny order. First, he asked me to lick his butthole. I only do that for Cody, but I was in no position to argue. Guilherme's ass was smooth and tan. It had no flavor, but the soft skin felt good against my lips. He rocked backward and forwards, his long penis swinging between his legs and hitting my bare chest. When I tried to put my tongue inside, he pulled away.

"Just the outside." I returned to licking his kid leather hiney. His penis no longer touched me. I couldn't see, but a quick brush of my hand told me he was hard, his big log of meat pointing straight out from his waist.

Guilherme tugged at my wrist. "Cody tells me you are an expert cocksucker."

Out loud, I said, "Yep." But inside, I thought, "Cody is a piece of shit."

Guilherme's cock had swelled up into a third leg. I put it in my mouth and slid it back to my tonsils. Guilherme didn't let me go deep. He kept it limited to just the first five inches. To my surprise, his hard dick continued to swell and stretch.

"This is it. That's my handsome cowboy." He lifted me by my armpits and threw me onto the round bed. Before I could protest, he had my legs in the air. He motioned to Cody, who picked up a tub labeled 'Oura, Oleina de Palma." I don't know what it was, but it was solid white, like a soap bar. As soon as it touched my skin, it turned into a clear oil.

The Oura made my ass so slick I couldn't stop Guilherme from putting his penis in my butt if I wanted to. I'd bet he's used to guys screaming when he puts it in. With my experience riding Cody's bull cock, Guilherme was a vacation. With Cody watching, I moaned and hung my arms over Guilherme's neck. I kissed his smooth chest and tongued his nipple.

"Ay, sim." Guilherme moaned. He was hitting the back of my rectum, just like he banged my tonsils earlier. Did he not know?

"You can go in all the way."

Guilherme frowned. "I am as far as I can go."

"No, silly, like this." I twisted my waist until the giant Brazilian cock slipped past the corner into my colon.

"Deus Meu!" The look on his face was priceless. He was gasping for air. "In my whole life, I never knew this was possible!"

"I hated seeing the base of your cock getting cold." I glanced over and saw Cody give a neutral stare, impossible to read. I decided he was super jealous and wanted me for his own. I kissed Guilherme and said, "Nobody does it better."

Guilherme chuckled, "Let's see if that is true." He pulled out suddenly, so my ass snapped shut. "Cody, he is all yours...for now."

Cody dropped his jeans, showing his knee-length soft dick.

Gruffly, he turned me so my head was dangling off the edge of the bed. Cody put his soft cock in my mouth. Like a hungry infant, I nursed on it until it grew and thickened. Cody thrust half his cock down my throat in one violent stab. I gagged and choked, but he didn't stop. He forced the rest until his pubic hair was tickling my chin. I couldn't breathe, but I didn't care if this was how Cody treated me. He pulled back, giving me one or two seconds of breath. Then he went deep and fucked my throat in small strokes. He blocked my airway. He closed his eyes and focused on his own pleasure, his cock swelling and stretching. I needed air. Cody's selfish pursuit of a full hard-on was going to kill me. I punched him hard in the abdomen. He yanked back, giving me my air, then punched me in the belly. It didn't hurt as much as my broken heart.

Without any tenderness, he put his cock against my hole. In one smooth motion, he filled me up completely, passing through the anus, the second sphincter, the rectum, the turn, and reaching deep into my sigmoid colon. And in the same swift movement, he withdrew until only his head filled my anus. He continued these long deep strokes, letting Guilherme see how much thicker and longer he was. Guilherme rubbed his crotch, keeping himself hard.

The Oura oil was so slippery there was no friction, only the sensation of a balloon filling with a hard cock. Guilherme came over and put his dick in Cody. Cody grimaced and said, "Ow, fuck!"

I said, "You can't take it, but you sure can dish it out."

Whatever was wrong between us had just gotten worse. My remark caused him to brutally fuck me without care, slamming into my butt and sphincters and pounding through the turn into the colon, only to yank his heavy cock head out, banging into barriers on the way out. I would have screamed in pain if it weren't for the Oura oil. I was lucky; it didn't hurt as much as Cody wanted.

"Is that all you got?" I was defiant and angry. Cody changed angles, so he was on top of me fucking down. That hurt. But I didn't realize what he was doing.

"Believe me, Brighton; I have something much worse for you."

I hated when anyone called me by that name. I couldn't see much except Cody's arm reaching behind him. Then I saw what he was doing and winced in terror. Cody had removed the Brazilian's cock from his ass, and now, it was brushing up against mine. Oiled up, I was powerless to stop them. I expected my skin to tear, but Guilherme slipped along Cody's cock into my already stretched hole without injuring me. I was in severe pain. I thrashed and screamed, but Cody put a hand over my mouth. I refused to cry. I made up my mind I was going to enjoy this no matter the pain. I was doing it to piss off Cody and to let Guilherme have his thousand-dollar sex.

In fractions of an inch, Guilherme added more of his fat cock to Cody's. My ass was spasming from the pain of being stretched. Cody pounded without mercy or care. Guilherme advanced until he reached the second sphincter. Here, it took him a lot to push through. I saw bright white lights when he did it. The pain was more than I could handle, but I pretended I was happy.

"Oh, two strong, handsome cowboys have their huge dicks in me at the same time! I'm the luckiest clown alive."

Then a minor miracle happened. Cody's thrusts were rubbing hard against Guilherme's cock. He had not begun fucking yet; he was still finding his way to my colon. The huge monster covering him and sliding all over his dick caused Guilherme to ejaculate.

Guilherme said, "Oh no! Oh, Cody, it's like you're fucking my pussy the way you rub me...oh, oh."

And my butt filled with Brazilian semen. Cody didn't stop; he continued to pound my insides. When the Brazilian's cock grew soft, it slipped out of me. I felt much better.

I turned to Cody and smiled. He leaned down and

whispered in my ear. "All of this is an act. Remember your part."

I ignored him and nibbled on his earlobe. "I'm changing the script."

I lay back and let the Caipirinha and the fucking carry me to the clouds. I writhed and moaned. "Cody, I love you. I love you so much." I spasmed when Cody filled me completely. "You're my man."

He raised a hand and said, "Fa—" he was going to call me a faggot, but something changed his mind. It was Guilherme. He was angry.

"What's wrong?" I asked our host.

Guilherme sighed. "It is so sad how much you love him, and he hates you back."

I turned to Cody. "Is it true? Do you hate me? I'm your little clown."

Cody gave in and put his mouth on mine, pressing past my lips with his huge tongue. We kept kissing until things became urgent. I broke the kiss when my cock began to throb on its own. Just knowing I was a perfect warm hole for Cody's enormous cock was enough to bring me to orgasm. I grunted. "Oh, crap. It's coming." And showers of white sperm landed on my forehead, my chin, the bed, and my belly.

Cody tilted his head back. "I'm close." I brushed the back of my hand against his nipples. It worked.

"Oh shit! Shit! Shit! Fuck Brightie, I'm coming." And he was. Cody's warm sperm filled my colon and rectum. He locked lips with me again. We stayed together. Cody was still hard inside me.

Guilherme stood and applauded. "The two lovebirds admit at last what I knew all along. Stay like that, don't move."

He ran to the kitchen and came back with a Brandy snifter. As Cody shrank, I pushed him out. Guilherme held the snifter below my stretched asshole and caught the first flood. I pushed hard, and a more powerful flood of mixed cum tumbled into the glass. He held it up.

"The elixir of life." He took a generous sip and handed the snifter to Cody. He took a swig. I finished it off.

Guilherme held the glass up. "Do you see the residue? If this glass were a woman, she would have sons with penises to their ankles."

We laughed at the absurdity.

❧ 41 ❧

ONE GROVER

The sunrise is hard to avoid in a house made of glass and concrete. Guilherme was in the kitchen making us a breakfast of coffee, french bread, and fruit from his garden. It wasn't like back home, but I knew better than to complain.

Guilherme pinched my cheeks and squeezed them together before kissing the top of my head. "You are such a beautiful boy; you must know that."

"No, sir. Back home, I would say I'm handsome. Beautiful's for girls."

This only made him laugh. He handed me coffee and bread. "The butter is on the table."

Cody joined us. Guilherme handed us each a very thin envelope. "American dollars, yes?"

It wasn't polite to count it out right there, but I figured it was okay to take a peek. I saw the words 'Will Pay to Bearer on Demand.' It was just one bill. That can't be right. I wanted to say something, but Cody made me stuff it in my pants pocket.

"What time is it?" I asked.

Guilherme smiled. "We are in the tropics, so you can tell from the light what time it is. The sun rises at 6:00 am and sets at 6:00 pm every day. It is now 7:00 am. I must be at the rodeo at 8:00. Is everybody ready?

Cody glared at his cup of coffee.

"You may bring this in the truck."

"I don't want to drink it out of my lap." He was tired and cranky, but it still came out good-natured. He took three big gulps and put it down on the counter.

"My staff will clean this up. Come, let's go."

The rodeo was just south of downtown, across from the hospital. Our hotel was within walking distance, but Cody wanted a cab. He acted distant and confused.

"Cody, how much did he pay us?"

"That's a thousand-dollar bill. Don't lose it. Hide it in your luggage."

I took it out and studied it.

"Who's that on the front?"

"Grover Cleveland."

We were scheduled to go on between the horses and the bulls. I hadn't met the other clowns yet. I was nervous, but I knew how to take charge as First Clown. They wouldn't understand a word I said, but they would get the most important stuff, like when I pointed or put my hand up. I could do this. In front of 12,000 people. Oh God, I had stage fright.

Cody slept most of the morning. I wanted to be near him, so I sat in the bathroom while he showered. At one point, he grabbed something that looked like a chrome snake with a garden spray nozzle head. He held it right in the crack of his ass. He let loose a light brown stream into the shower. He repeated it several times until only clear water came out.

"You will do this from now on."

I wondered why he would talk to me like that. Cody said, "I told you, boy, you're my property. I need you to keep the important parts clean."

It was like someone else had visited him and decided to stay inside his head. My Cody was tender, loving, devoted to me in every way. I left the bathroom before he finished drying himself so he wouldn't see the tears. I wiped my face on the pillow and put on my baggy overalls. Once my eyes were dried, and Cody was strutting about naked, knocking stuff over with his big ass and huge cock, I applied my makeup. Cody acted like I wasn't even in the room.

I had to say something, but it was not the right time. Cody was in a terrible mood. What had I done? It was time to focus on fighting off the bull and to leave Cody in a place in my mind where emotions didn't matter. I needed to protect him. I focused my memories on the good times, before this other person showed up.

Hands clamped around my throat from behind. Cody pulled me close, choking me. "You're going to let me blow another load in your ass right now." He was still naked, and his hard cock was resting on my shoulder.

"Cody, I got my makeup on. I can't."

I removed my overalls and the rest. I sat on the bed, waiting for him to fuck me.

"Brightie, what did I tell you?" He pointed toward the bathroom.

After my shower washed away all my hard work, I put the nozzle into my hole and sprayed it. Gobs of leftover cum were all that came out on the first try. The second time, I felt a rumbling which meant I was cleaning my colon. I waited, then danced over to the toilet. The third one was brown water. The fourth one was clear, but I just kept going, hoping to avoid Cody's mean fucking. I tried something new. I filled my rectum with water, then opened my sphincter without removing the hose. I was deep cleaning the walls. It felt so damn good, I didn't notice when Cody stormed in. He put me in a headlock and dragged me onto the bed.

He was already greased with Albolene. He forced his monster into my unwilling asshole with no kissing or tenderness. He pounded very hard, very fast, very deep. It was more painful than having two men in me at once. It was like the violent sex was meant to punish me. Problem was that I liked it, like Br'er Rabbit in the briar patch. Cody was just fucking me for his own pleasure, so I kept mine hidden from him. I let the clear sticky stuff fill my palm. When his eyes were closed, I ate the evidence. Cody's cock was punching my colon, not just filling it. He pounded hard, giving me that horrible, not-right feeling a dozen times.

"Cody, you're hurting me."

"And you like it, you little faggot. I saw you lick your jizz." He pounded in a different rhythm that meant he was close to climax. "You'd better come, Brightie. I won't be the only one, you hear?"

I nodded. I played with a nipple and sinfully stroked my dick, remembering all the good sex in the past. It was working.

Cody threw his head back and sprayed load after load of angry semen into my butthole. When it was my turn, I aimed my cock at his face. My sperm hit him in his eyes, his nose, and his mouth. Served him right.

"Go clean out my spunk."

Cody's soft cock was covered in my blood. A trickle of blood and semen leaked out of my stretched hole. Cody went white.

"Oh shit, Brightie, I'm so sorry. I was playing a game. Oh, no!"

I shrugged. It was all I could say.

When I went to clean out my ass, some semen and a lot of blood stained the water. Cody came in and sat on the toilet. I was in shock. I just kept rinsing, but more blood came.

"Brightie, I don't know why I'm acting like this."

I dried off, leaving blood on the towel. "Well, it started after I made a joke about you killing people."

Cody covered his face. "I don't want to be like this with you. I'm so ashamed." He cried.

I didn't try to comfort him. I reapplied my clown

makeup. I was still leaking blood, so I wadded up some toilet paper and stuffed it in my buttcrack.

"We need to get you to the hospital."

"I gotta perform with you in two hours. The hospital is right across the street. I'll go there myself afterward."

Cody punched himself in the head a half dozen times. "Why did I turn on the most lovely, caring, and sexy man I have ever known?"

I knew a good story to help. "My momma had this high school friend who she really liked. That friend, Myrna, had a bunch of real bad news all in a short time. She lost her only living Grandma of natural causes. Her parents died in an accident with her only brother. She was alone, and it was high school, so the county showed up and sent her off to a home because she was seventeen."

Cody leaned forward.

"So she comes back to town in the summer. Momma was able to convince her folks to let Myrna stay with them. Myrna was so close with momma, but then all of a sudden, she turned on her over nothing. She ran away and stayed with relatives. But she fought with them and ran away again to see Momma, but her folks said she couldn't stay. Myrna ended it right there. She left town, and no one knows where she is."

Cody frowned. "That's a sad story. Why did you tell it?"

"Well, Momma couldn't understand why she lost her friend. She was real tore up and went to talk to a counselor about it. The counselor says that Myrna had lost so much that she loved she was afraid to love anyone again. So she fights with them and pushes them away because she loves them and because she's scared of getting hurt again."

When I turned away from my makeup mirror, Cody had his head in his hands. He was sobbing. He wiped the tears from his eyes, blew his nose, then hugged me the way he normally does.

"Brightie, you are so smart. I will never mistreat you like that again. No more violence, and no more ordering you around."

"You can order me around any time, sir. And a little violence is fun. Just not too much."

Cody chuckled. "Then get those fucking clown overalls on, boy. We got a show to put on."

"Yes, sir" I couldn't hide my boner.

✤ 42 ✤
THE BIG SHOW

Back home, the rodeo ring was just that: a ring. From where I was standing, this rodeo was long and wide, like a rounded -football field. I was standing on the fifty-yard line. This was a mixed bless-ing. It meant that there were more places for Cody to get away from the bull. It also meant I had a lot farther to run if Cody was in trouble. That was the situation.

A few minutes earlier, I was backstage with the Second Clown and the Barrel. The second clown was named Jawan, spelled Joao. Joao was tall and lanky. He had green eyes and Brazilian-colored skin that turned brown, not red, in the sun.

The barrel clown was named Paulo. He was short and squat, just like a barrel. His skin was very dark. He wore long, straight black hair pulled into a ponytail. He looked like an Indian with black skin. Paulo didn't speak English; Joao did, just barely.

Because Joao was my backup, I needed to make sure we had our signals right. We reviewed fists and fingers and the cutthroat. I was relieved that most of them meant the same thing. I was worried that there was no sign for me to transfer responsibility to the Second or the Barrel. In Brazil, the First Clown was always in charge unless he was knocked out. They used a signal flipping the middle finger, which meant 'watch your back.' My signal for 'rider down to your left,' a smack to the left wrist with your hand in a fist, meant the same thing in Brazil as the middle finger did back home.

When we entered the arena, the loudspeaker erupted in gibberish. The only words I understood were 'America,' 'Cody Cameron,' and 'Texas.' Then I heard my name and applause, so I bowed.

Cody sat on a white Bull whose name was lost in all the Portuguese. He prepped his rope with rosin and tied it down. I saw him nod firmly, confident he was going to dazzle the audience. He wasn't wrong.

A loud buzzer sounded, and the gate flew open. The bull, who I named 'Whitie' to rhyme with Brightie, was perfect. He spun to the right, giving Cody enough balance to use his spurs, front-back, and front-back. The audience roared. Cody's hat stayed on his head through the whole ride. When the eight-second buzzer sounded, Cody released his rope and gracefully landed on his feet. Twelve thousand people yelled and leaped to their feet, applauding wildly. Cody removed his hat and bowed.

I put myself between him and Whitie. That bull was not gonna let my cowboy walk away easy. Like a bull in a Bugs Bunny cartoon, Whitie scratched the dirt with his front hoof and snorted steam.

My signals worked; Joao, the Second Clown, joined me. Together we waved our arms to distract him, then split up to divide his attention.

"Good job, clown." Cody winked at me and jogged toward the side of the arena. Watching his ass move in those jeans was like getting drunk. I turned away from my distraction to see Joao lying on the ground. What had happened? The barrel clown was making the children laugh; he didn't notice. I got his attention and made the sign for 'man down.' Paulo's barrel followed behind him as he turned and gave me the finger. I knew this was going to happen. He thinks I flipped him off. But he held the finger steady. I remembered it meant 'behind you.' I didn't have time to turn. Horns pierced my giant overalls. In a split second, I was six feet above the ground, caught between the bull's horns. The crowd let out a gasp.

Even in my panic, my first concern was Joao. I didn't know how badly he was hurt. I twisted my head and saw the second clown on his feet, dusting off his jeans. When he saw me, horror spread across his face. I think all this happened in less than a second.

The bull was determined to get me off his horns. He threw his head back, and I came loose as I somersaulted through the air, landing on Whitie's back. The stadium cheered and thundered applause. Great. How was I going to jump off this bull without dying?

Whitie charged straight for Paulo, who turtled into the barrel. The bull struck hard, and Paulo went flying, rolling until he smacked a wall. I knew he was okay, having done barrel myself. They're like a feather pillow inside.

Whitie was bucking angrily, desperate to buck me off. I held his neck and scratched behind one of his ears. He stopped and leaned his head in so I could scratch harder. He kicked one of his rear legs the way a dog might kick when you rub his belly.

Without warning, Whitie took off running to the far end of the stadium. His run became a canter, then a slow trot. He turned and trotted straight down the middle of the arena. I didn't need to hold on tight now. I raised one arm, holding Whitie's hump for balance with the other. The stadium went mad. Whitie headed for the exit chute. As I passed by the staging area, one of the cowboys grabbed my raised arm and lifted me to safety. When he did, I heard another gasp of horror from the stadium. Below me, Whitie's back was stained red with blood. I turned to thank the cowboy who rescued me. It was Cody. I was dizzy. "Did I do okay, sir?"

Cody said nothing. He didn't have to. His face was a mix of pride and guilt. I was so cold on a hot day. I leaned into Cody and said, "I love you, Daddy."

He fought back tears and said, "I love you too, my little clown." I planted my lips on his for a kiss before the world went bright red, then black.

❦ 43 ❧
BED REST

The blackness changed to bright white. I couldn't see yet, but I could feel and hear. I was lying down in a bed. Someone held my hand. It was Cody. I could smell him. He smelled like a man. Not just any man. The man I loved.

"Hey, little clown."

"Hospital?" I asked.

"Yup."

"Same doctor?"

"Nope."

I sighed with relief. "Good."

The room came into focus. I saw Joao, Paulo, and Guilherme too. Guilherme spoke.

"The clowns wish to offer their apologies for failing you."

"I had the best performance of my life. They didn't fail me."

Guilherme spoke in rapid Portuguese to the two stricken men. Their frowns melted into smiles when they understood I was grateful, not mad.

"What happened after?" I asked Cody.

"After what?"

"The last thing I remember is someone pulling me

off the bull by my arm. Wait, it was you. I kissed you in front of ten thousand people, didn't I?"

Guilherme interjected. "This is Brazil. All men kiss one another. It's a greeting. Or a kiss of gratitude."

Cody nodded. "This country is so much more open."

"What did the doctor say?"

"This doctor believes the bull must have damaged your internal organs."

I shot a knowing glare at Cody and said, "Yeah, the bull did. But then he repented and changed his tune. You all saw."

Cody wiped his brow. "Yeah, that bull sure likes you. I'll bet if he could say he was sorry, he would."

"He already did."

I had lost a lot of blood. The whole town wanted to donate their blood for me. I was a hero to them all. The clown who tamed the wild bull. It will make great stories for grandkids. I wonder if they will leave in the kiss? Probably not.

I saw the Barrel Clown. "Thank you, Paulo."

He said something that sounded like, "Gee, not a...."

Joao said something rapid in Portuguese. Guilherme translated. "Working under such a noble and talented First Clown is an honor." Ass kisser.

"Obrigado, Joao." My first attempt at speaking Portuguese.

"Gee, not a..."

I turned back to Cody. "How long until I can...until we can—"

Cody shook his head. "Unless we change the official story, we won't know."

Guilherme butted in.

"There is a clinic for men like us in Sao Paulo. I will have you seen as soon as they let you go."

I frowned. "Until I can go?"

Cody avoided my eyes. "The bull did a lot of damage. It's going to be a week before you can leave."

"I sure hope that bull is sorry for what he did."

Sadness and guilt covered his face. He nodded.

❧ 44 ❧

MAURO

After living out in the country, working every day on the farm, and driving all over creation, it was hard for me to accept bed rest. They made me do my business in a bedpan, which is basically a metal toilet lid with a box under it. I had to stay in bed to do a number one or a number two. The doctor checked my poop for blood content. She said that I could go once there were three days in a row with no "fecal occult blood." It sounds like witchcraft to me.

The best part of being stuck there was how Cody never left my side until I fell asleep for the night. Guilherme put me in a private room where the nurses always knocked, so we had a lot of time alone.

One of the nurses was a man named Mauro. He had creamy brown skin, so light it was almost white. His dark brown hair, parted in the middle, framed a fine-looking face. Like a Latino James Dean. Above his lip, he had a dark peach-fuzz mustache. His dark eyes sparkled whenever he saw us together. I never saw a male nurse's uniform before. It was baggy, but when he bent or walked, it was very revealing. The cotton fabric jiggled when he walked. If he bent down, his round ass might as well be bare. When he reached up high, his pecker was swinging under those pants. He spoke perfect English because he had spent his childhood in Miami. We had to watch our language with him.

On the fourth night since the rodeo, I felt awful uncomfortable. It's like until I had sex, I never knew what I was missing. But now that I had, I needed it something terrible. My balls hurt, and I kept popping boners.

"Cody, I can't stop getting hard-ons, and my balls hurt. Is something wrong?"

"You got blue balls."

There was a knock on the door. "May I come in?" It was Mauro.

He changed my bedpan and fluffed my pillows.

"Can I get you or your friend anything else?" He cocked his head to one side like the RCA Victor dog.

"Uh, no thanks, Mauro."

"Are you sure?"

He didn't point, but his eyes fell on my blanket, sticking up like a tent. I was so embarrassed.

"Oh god, Mauro, I don't mean nothing by it."

"Is it because of this?" He bent down and showed off his round bottom. "Or maybe because of this?" He shook his hips side to side, and I watched his dick flop underneath the fabric.

"Stop! You're making it worse!" I was leaking pre-cum, and my blanket had a spot.

"Oh, you're drooling!" Mauro laughed.

Cody didn't say a word.

Mauro continued, "I can help you, but I can't help your friend very much." He indicated a growing stain on Cody's leg. He was blue balls too, and I couldn't do nothing about it.

"Come, I will help you. It's cool, right?"

Cody agreed.

"I will help you, and you will help him." He made a funny gesture with his fist, tongue, and cheek that was supposed to look like he had a small cock in his mouth.

I misunderstood what he was saying. He wanted me to suck Cody, but he had something much more elaborate for me. Mauro used a special key to lock the door from the inside.

Oh god, that ass shook so good when he walked to the door, and his dick was such a tease in those pants. I prepared for him to go down on me.

"Stop, don't touch anything. Let Nurse Mauro heal you."

He kicked off his shoes, climbed onto the bed, lowered the blanket, and lifted my hospital gown. He gasped with delight. I forgot it's pretty big. You tend to forget that when you're with Cody.

"Oh, perfect! It's a dick made for fucking." Mauro brought out a tube of clear jelly and added a nozzle. He put the tube inside himself and squeezed. He shivered.

"Ooh, cold!" I will only give you a little. He put some in his hand and was about to put it on my dick when Cody stood, arms folded.

"Hey! He can't have any pressure there."

Cody stood within arm's reach, so I undid his belt buckle.

Mauro laughed. "I have a solution." He pointed to the ceiling.

We both looked up. There were ropes and pulleys that the doctors used to keep broken limbs up in the air. He put the cold gel on my hard wiener and stroked it a couple of times.

Cody wasn't satisfied, but he stepped closer to me so I could unbutton his fly with my mouth. I bit the fly and, with my teeth, pulled, one button at a time, until he was fully undone. His pants fell, and his big balls swung forward and bounced against my nose. It was heaven. I wished we could do that over and over.

Above me, Mauro had freed up the traction device and was looping the ropes in an elaborate pattern. I watched, fascinated by the contraption but also because I saw his cute dick bouncing in those pants.

Cody wasn't sure. "He can't be bucking or fucking, Mauro."

Mauro winked. "He won't; you will see."

I used my index fingers to loosen both legs of Cody's jeans. I spent extra time on his left leg, where the jeans fabric had become trapped between his big thighs and cock. I freed it up, and the pants dropped to his ankles. Cody was soft but growing.

Mauro took his shirt off and pushed those pants down, stepping out of them. Completely naked, he looked even better than before. His butt was rounder, smoother, and more meaty. It wasn't just the pants; Mauro was a damned handsome nurse.

I lifted Cody and put the soft head of his penis in my mouth. I sucked and nursed like a calf until the long tube of meat straightened out and stiffened. I wished I had cocaine at that moment. Mauro reached into his discarded pants pocket and handed me a tiny bottle of throat spray made from cocaine.

"You will need this."

He was right. I forgot how violently Cody had fucked my throat the last time. I loved it, but it still would hurt. I sprayed a few times, and the mist settled on my tonsils and the back of my throat.

"Swallow some. Not too much."

I sprayed a few more times until it gathered in a pool at the back of my throat. I sat forward, and the solution ran down my throat, numbing everything in its path. My heart rate increased, and my need for sex tripled. I wanted Cody in me. I wanted him to fuck my butt, but this time the throat would have to do.

I glanced up and saw Mauro sitting, dangling from the rope contraption. His heart-shaped butt was exposed, and his legs were hooked in stirrups. He had good back support. Then he pressed a metal brake, and he came lowering slowly towards me. He had positioned himself perfectly; I could see his butthole quivering with anticipation. It opened like a little mouth yawning.

Cody watched skeptically, fearing Mauro would come crashing down on me, reopening my injuries. The cocaine had awakened an animal in my soul. I needed Cody somewhere deep inside me. I pushed until his head was in. He rubbed the back of my throat, and I swallowed him in giant gulps, so he vanished down my numb throat. He took his eyes off Mauro and looked at me. I was completely stuffed from my mouth to my chest. Mauro watched in amazement.

"Brightie, you are so talented. No one else could do this." He probably didn't know he was right. Cody had found the one man, a rodeo clown, who could take him completely at both ends. He let out a whisper. "Oh, Brightie, I love you."

I would have answered him if I had any air and a place to release it.

He humped my mouth, pulling back to my tonsils so I could breathe, and waited several breaths before going deep and jackhammering his tool along the tight sides of my throat.

Just then, a warm, soft butt touched my penis. When I saw it, I got even harder. He put two fingers on my dick to position it, then continued to lower himself. With Cody sliding in and out of my mouth, Mauro squeezing my dick with his tight bottom, and cocaine coursing through me, I was in a place I wished I could stay forever. I thought about asking Cody if we could bring Mauro home with us. It was just a passing thought brought on by drugs. Besides, I couldn't ask if I wanted to. My mouth and throat were busy doing their job.

I watched Mauro as he reached the widest part of my dick. He stopped for a second and, clicking another brake, reversed direction. I was disappointed, but he lowered himself again, backed off, and then moved the whole way down so his smooth butthole touched my pubic hair.

"Oh fuck, you're big!" Mauro said. I know he could see Cody, who dwarfed every man on the planet, but he still meant it. Using the two brakes, he raised and lowered his improvised device, stretching his butthole, making it less resistant. On one trip up, he let my cock go. I saw his ass, which had stretched like a vagina, and a gaping hole that slowly contracted into a winking, puckered eye. He landed right on me, and I went back up inside. The movement was slow and steady. I needed to come so bad; whether he went fast or slow didn't matter. My dick was already a fountain of clear fluid. The fountain wound up inside Mauro, providing a more human lubricant. Mauro's penis was beautiful. It was smaller than most, but its shape was perfect. Droplets of pre-ejaculate formed at the little pee hole. Without warning, they gushed and became a sticky spiderweb connecting my belly to his dick. Mauro's eyes were closed. He was saying prayers of thanks under his breath.

I turned my attention back to Cody. I couldn't feel anything because of the cocaine, but I tasted his pre-cum on my tongue. I looked up into his eyes, and they said he was close. He made a low growl that grew louder as he came closer. I pulled him all the way out to tell him just one thing.

"It won't hurt, so don't hold back, Cody."

He grew more violent, but it was just like I had requested: a little violence. He came to the head of the bed so my upside-down mouth and throat would make a straight line for him to use. He pulled very far out and plunged deep - pubes to whiskers. It didn't hurt in the least. Because he was taking long strokes, I had plenty of time to catch a breath before he blocked my airway again. I held my breath and took air on every fifth stroke, like how they taught us in swimming lessons. Cody closed his eyes, heading into the home stretch.

More strings of sticky hot pre-cum dribbled on my belly. Mauro rode me like a Ferris wheel. Up, up, up; down, down, down. It was so consistent; it pushed me very close to the edge.

"You like this, Brightie?"

I nodded as best I could with a pole down my throat. Then, hands-free, Mauro sprayed all three of us with his cum. There was so much of it we all got soaking wet. He lowered himself completely and used the pulsing of his never-ending orgasm to squeeze my cock at the base. I could only make a little noise, but it was my signal that I was gonna come.

At that moment, a flood of fluid shot down my throat into my stomach. Cody thrashed and bucked, feeding me a meal's worth of his salty semen. With his cock firing hot white sperm inside me, I hit my peak. I touched Mauro's perfect ass and adorable penis. He shivered, then moaned as my cock delivered its load inside him.

"Oh, Brightie! Oh God! You get so huge when you come. Oh, ow!"

Cody's cock flopped out of my mouth. He bent down to kiss me and slurped up some of his own sperm. Next, Cody pulled Mauro to him and put his mouth over the handsome nurse's stretched-out pussy of an ass. He sucked my sperm out. He missed its taste, I figured. He bent down and kissed me again, giving me a taste of my own sperm. Then he kissed Mauro, and the circle was complete.

Before Mauro came down out of his clever contraption, Cody whispered in his ear. Mauro shook his head three times in a row. Then he shrugged and agreed.

Cody asked permission, which was the right thing to do. He had talked Mauro into taking him as far as he could go, I was jealous at first, but when I stopped to think, it would be good and fair for Cody to come inside a man other than me. Here was the perfect opportunity.

Cody wheeled my bed backward and sat himself on a rolling metal chair. His long floppy cock swung in lazy circles like a horse's. I watched with jealousy and curiosity as Cody rubbed himself hard. It wasn't as hard as with me, I told myself. From where I sat and the way he leaned back in the chair, his cock was higher than his cowboy hat. Mauro didn't have very far to drop before he reached the tip. He made the sign of the cross and guided the head into his stretchy asshole. It was surprising how much it looked like a vagina. In a way, it was.

Mauro let out some very quiet screams as gravity forced his anus to accept Cody's fist-sized cockhead. Tears came out of his eyes. I didn't want Cody to see that. Luckily, he had his head back, smiling at me. He winked.

Mauro kept descending, impaling himself inch-by-painful inch. With each inch, Cody's cock narrowed a little more, and Mauro smiled. When he hit the second sphincter, Mauro hid his distress and let Cody through. At the back wall, he sighed and changed direction. He didn't even have half of Cody in him. But I judged too soon. He came down again, leaning in his swing, and let Cody tear through his butt until he reached the colon. There, it was only a matter of allowing the huge cock to slide forward. I could see Cody's cock head protruding as it made its way through the sigmoid colon. When Mauro saw it, he smiled even harder. With great satisfaction, he landed in Cody's lap. They didn't kiss, but I could see they wanted to.

"Go ahead; it's part of the magic." I didn't feel as generous as that sounded.

Mauro and Cody kissed passionately. I gripped the

sheets, frustrated. I knew that my ass was a better fit, but Mauro, with help, was able to ride the flagpole. Seeing Cody kiss someone else, balls deep in their shitter, I felt pushed aside like my bed.

Then he surprised me. He stopped kissing Mauro and reached for me. His eyes were wet.

Just then, there came a sharp knock at the door. Cody winced when Mauro's ass clenched involuntarily. A female nurse shouted something in Portuguese. Mauro shouted back. She left.

He spoke to Cody, not me, and said, "She needs to give medicine to Brightie. I told her I was in the middle of changing his clothing."

We had only a few minutes. Let me correct that. They had only a few minutes. I could just fake sleep. Cody was rock hard, and it didn't seem like Mauro was prepared for the reverse fuck. It hurts much worse. As he pressed the brake that lifted him skyward, Cody rolled back in his chair. When Cody was partway out, Mauro let out a scream. It wasn't quiet. I knew that must be Cody's cockhead squeezing through the tiny exit from the colon. I grinned, thinking how I mastered all that on the first day up in Laramie. Another scream. I saw Cody was still rock hard and was pretty far along. I waited for the next shout. It was the sphincter that divides the rectum from the anus, what I call the second hole. One tight spot left, the butthole, but I forgot how loose Mauro was. Cody slipped out like a Polish sausage falling off a table.

45

RODEO HEROES

I forgave Mauro, especially when I considered all the hard work he put into getting me off. They released me after six days. It was Friday. To my embarrassment, someone must have told the town where to find me. There were hundreds of well-wishers outside with flowers. Children asked me for my autograph. Paulo and Joao hugged me and gave me little Brazilian flags on thick black flagpoles. Guilherme stood at the top of the steps and made a short, powerful speech. He gestured wide towards me several times and Cody once or twice. Cody was listening intently. In his ear, I asked what he was saying.

Cody translate. "He says that a true hero rarely appears. The rodeo brings heroes from near and far. Something about magic or magical, you are a hero, I am a hero, as a clown, you're a hero who rescues other heroes, so you're the most heroic, and yet the most humble as well. That is a true hero. After that, he switched to some local business about an election. Oh wait, he wants us to come forward."

Cody and I stepped to Guilherme's side and bowed on cue. The crowd cried out as one. It sounded like nonsense, but I managed to filter out the noise and discovered they were shouting in unison, "Brightie! Cody! Brightie! Cody!" I was never called a hero before, and I never heard anyone so much as announce me on a loud-speaker. But here in Barretos, I was Elvis.

✣ 46 ✣

INTERNAL APPRAISAL

Guilherme was a man of his word. When we reached Sao Paulo, the driver stopped at a clinic in an expensive neighborhood. The doctor and a nurse came right to the car to greet me. Guilherme must have paid him good. They wheeled me into a private room on the tenth floor. I had a view of the endless forest of buildings, new construction, and cranes. Cody waited while I talked with the doctor. His English was easy to understand. He gave me some injections that made my head fuzzy. I stripped and put on a hospital gown. I do not like those things. But I guess they make life easy for the doctor. From under the table, he raised some metal stirrups, and I put my bare feet in them. They were cold and awkward. My dick and balls covered my asshole, so the doctor used a strap to keep them out of the way.

"Brightie, tell me how you were injured." I swallowed. "You are among friends here, son."

"Okay, well, Cody made a mistake, but he knows it."

The doctor leaned in. "Can you be more specific, please?"

I jumped when cold jelly squirted up inside me. The doctor took a gloved finger and worked it in. He pressed somewhere that made me trickle pre-come. It felt good. I sighed and continued. "Okay, he was not himself. I know he didn't mean to."

"You aren't answering the question."

"He fucked me hard. It was not like the good kind; it was like he was punishing or beating me."

The doctor inserted something cold and metal and began examining my butt. I couldn't see him or the device, but I could tell it was like a snake.

"I see a lot of healing skin in your rectum, and your sphincters were torn. They are healing fine." He paused and cleared his throat. "I am guessing he is of above-average dotage."

Huh?

"Oh, I mean, he is huge."

"The biggest."

"Yes, I see he tore your rectal valve and bruised your rectosigmoid junction. Less than 1% of all penises are long enough to do this."

"I'll bet."

I heard the doctor catch his breath. "This isn't possible. What did he use to do this to you?"

"I beg your pardon?"

"There are healing fissures in your sigmoid colon, but also at the bottom of your descending colon."

"Yep."

"I will repeat my question to you. What did Cody insert in you? A broom? A penis could not possibly cause this damage. You are the victim. You don't have to explain."

"But --"

The doctor pressed a button, and the nurse appeared.

Cody snarled. This already happened in Barretos. Don't doctors talk to each other?

The doctor stood and removed his gloves.

"You have frightened this boy from telling the truth. What did you use to sodomize him?"

Cody unbuttoned his jeans and pushed them past his knees. They fell to his ankles. His huge soft cock swung like a pendulum, bouncing between each knee.

The doctor sucked air between his teeth. "Unusual. Now I make the connection."

"Shall I?" Cody gestured towards his jeans.

The doctor's jaw went slack. It was pretty astonishing the first time. He didn't look away until Cody stuffed every inch down his pant leg and buttoned up.

Returning to me, he put on a fresh pair of gloves, added some KY, and retracted the device. He stopped and tapped the walls of my digestive system at places where I was torn or bruised. He smiled.

"This is all healing, and there is no sepsis." The doctor smiled.

"So can we?"

He turned away. "It is dangerous. To be safe, I would recommend another week. Even then, it may be very painful. From now on, Cody must be a gentle lover with you. I am still not sure it is healthy for you to host him, er, take him inside you. It is too abnormal."

Hearing those words was shocking, but the expression on Cody's face was enough to break my heart. He was so hurt, angry, and ashamed.

❧ 47 ❧

DARK SECRETS

When the fuzzy-headed medicine wore off, a bottle came uncorked. In the car to our hotel, I cried like a baby. Cody held me and rubbed my hair. I knew I was completely safe. Because of all the other cars, our car moved along slower than a stubborn mule. I gazed up at him.

"Cody, you know I ain't never leaving you. I'll heal up fine. You know how to do it normal and not violent."

Cody hung his head. "It's too risky. If I killed you like I...if I killed you, it would be the end of me."

I understood his logic, but I didn't believe it. I knew how to fix this. "Cody, in your life, how many times have you fucked someone violently?"

"Twice."

And how many times have you fucked somebody not violently?

He was counting on his hands. "Maybe thirty times?"

"Most of those times was me, right?"

Cody's brow creased. "Yeah."

I decided to address the unspoken problem. "You killed someone once, didn't you?"

He didn't say anything.

"Was he as good at this as me?"

Cody surprised me. "No, she wasn't." My whole picture of life before Brightie took a turn.

"I didn't realize."

Cody needed to say it. "I was young, Brightie, about your age, and I didn't have a clue what I was doing, nor that my huge dick made me a freak. Every girl in school broke up with me and never said why. I was a virgin. I knew I was big, but nobody could help me with the problem. You don't talk about that stuff out loud. I might as well have had no dick at all because it was the cause of all my problems. Sorry, I'm jumping back and forth a bit."

"No problem. I've been dying to hear this since we met."

"So the richest family in Fort Worth was somehow made aware of my predicament. They had a daughter who fucked everything in sight. She was insatiable. I think it was an illness."

This was getting strange. "Go on."

"So the family contacts me and asks me to dinner. I thought maybe it was a job offer or something. So we're sitting in the den, just the mother and father, and they get right to the point. They said they heard about my 'endowment' and wanted me to marry their daughter, provided the rumors were true."

"What?"

"I know, it's weird. Money makes people weird. Like a bull at the county fair, I had to strip and show them my soft cock, and then get it hard. The father nearly fainted. He touched it under the pretense of 'making sure it was real,' but I knew part of him wanted some of this dick." Cody grabbed his left leg to add emphasis.

"That's not normal."

"Nothing about my dick is normal, as you already know. Anyway, while I'm standing there, this sex-crazed daughter walks into the room and screams. I lost my hard-on. She was beautiful, with dark hair, like a young

Elizabeth Taylor. And her tits were huge. It was like I had won a game show or something."

I was jealous, but it was over a woman, so it didn't hurt much.

"Anyway, they say I have the right equipment to keep her happy and worn out. They want the wedding as soon as possible. The local papers knew about Linda, and the parents didn't want a bunch of scandals alongside the wedding announcement. They planned to have it in Key West. It was far away, and that town is well known for turning a blind eye to scandal.

"My folks came and were as confused as I had been. I didn't tell them what was really going on."

"Cody, this is a strange tale."

He didn't look at me, but he smiled. "The wedding was small, and we were happy. She was the first girl who hadn't pushed me away after discovering my giant dick. We went up to the hotel room to consummate the marriage, even though every man in Fort Worth and Dallas had already consummated her. She could only take about half of me, but she did it well. I blew my first load inside her, and it was perfect.

"I got up to shower. Soaping myself off, I heard the phone ring. When I came back into the room, she was just finishing the call. Something was wrong, but she said nothing. She wiped away tears, smiled, and dragged me into the bed for round two. She rubbed her titties on my dick, and I got hard. She grabbed the end of my dick and shoved it in her pussy, then pulled me by the ass so I slammed into her over and over. She was hurting herself. I tried to stop her. She was screaming out for me to fuck her hard, harder! Her vagina was deep, but not deep enough.

"When she realized six inches of my dick were still in the open air, she pounded on my chest. She stood, turned around, and sat down hard on my cock. Her asshole was pretty loose for a girl, I think."

I laughed, but Cody's expression grew dark.

"Even before I had fully penetrated her, I saw blood. It was coming from her pussy. She had done damage there. She forced me deep in her ass and tore herself to pieces until the whole bed was covered in blood. Despite that awful blood, I still came in her ass, and she rolled off me."

I thought I knew what was coming next, but I didn't. "Did she die?"

"First, she thanked me. She told me that fucking helps her shut down her emotions. My beautiful, gigantic cock fucked away all her feelings, and she needed to stop feeling. She said I was the perfect husband and we would be happy together. Then she told me about the phone call."

"Oh shit."

Cody's eyes were wet. He wiped them with the sleeve of his shirt. "Uhm -- so the call was from the airport. The flight from Key West back to Dallas hit some bad weather. Her folks and my folks went down in the Gulf of Mexico, along with all our Texas relatives, which was pretty much everyone. Linda sent me to the corner to buy some rum. We got plastered. I blacked out having more rough sex with her. When I woke up, I was an orphan, a millionaire, and a widower. The sex that night had been too much for her, and she bled out."

"Holy crap, Cody. No wonder you're -- that's more burden than any man should bear."

"The Key West cops suspected murder. I had to show them my penis and explain as best I could. The autopsy confirmed that my huge dick caused her death. They charged me with involuntary manslaughter, but Fred Rossi, the DA, came to me in jail and said he would drop the charges...if I agreed to meet him later at his house."

I knew where this was going.

"I was released, and I kept my word. Fred, the DA, had a nice big house in the rich part of town. He answered the door in a bathrobe. I walked in, and he caught me off guard. He pushed me into a sofa. He wanted to see it, like everybody else. I was a god-damned prize bull at the county fair. But I took off my pants and showed him the murder weapon.

"I felt dirty, ashamed, guilty. Fred was very kind. Kinder than anyone I'd met in my life. He told me I had an extraordinary gift and would someday learn how to use it safely."

I scoffed. "I did not see that coming."

Cody smiled. "He asked if I had ever taken a man inside me. When I said no, he showed me how to do it. He was the first man to come inside me. It was addictive. All the responsibility and fear drained away, and I let the older man do all the work. He held my cock in his hands while he fucked me and took more than one faceful of my cum that night.

"Fred knew all the best attorneys and helped me protect my sudden inheritance in investments and gold. He didn't need my money, and attorney-client privilege meant he didn't know how much it was."

"How much was it?"

"If I tell you, you have to promise not to tell anyone."

I nodded.

"It was sixty million dollars. It's more than that now, thanks to Fred's advice."

I breathed out. Cody wasn't rich. He was fucking rich. "I'll bet you feel better now that you got that story off your chest."

Cody smirked. "It isn't quite over. See, in my mind, I didn't have violent sex with Linda; she had violent sex with me."

"Oh, no."

"Oh yes, Brightie. My relationship with Fred was

long-distance. I was riding bulls and building my home in McKinney; he worked in Florida. I often bought him a ticket to come and fuck. He was happy to drop a few loads in me and fly home to Florida. I wanted more. I spent thousands in long-distance phone calls, sweet talking him and planning to pounce when the time was right.

"One hot night in June, he flew to Dallas to give me the in, out, leave. I told him it wasn't gonna be like that. I told him he was staying for a week. When he tried to go, I pinned him to the wall and kissed him. He looked at me differently. I thought maybe I had killed our relationship. I had only changed it. Fred wanted me to fuck him.

"That was when I first learned about Albolene. Fred was a passive homosexual, so he was used to the pain of being fucked. He didn't do as well as you, Brightie, but he did manage to let me in partway. If I tried to go deeper, he pounded his fists on my chest, so I backed off. I was terrified after what had happened before, so I was super gentle with him. Although I couldn't go all the way like I do with you, at least I could come inside him."

I tried to hide the jealousy, but Cody saw it and shook his head. "There's more. He was my first. I thought he would be my one and only. Summer ended. He came up in October and said he couldn't stay long. I shrugged. No biggie, right? I fuck him and come inside him, and then, before I was even out, he breaks up with me. He met a woman, and he wants to marry her. That was when the sex turned violent. I thought that if I couldn't have him ever again, I could at least have him all the way. I didn't care that he was screaming while I pushed all the way in his shitter. I didn't care that I saw blood. It couldn't hurt as much as the betrayal. I came and came again, fucking him without mercy."

I rubbed Cody's arm consolingly.

"When my supply of cum ran out, and my rage had passed, the color had drained out of Fred. I saw blood on the bed. It was a nightmare. It was Linda all over again. I didn't know what I could do."

"Did you go to jail?" I asked.

Cody shook his head. "Fred was still in love with me, or he would never have done what he did. He said he was fine, to please call a taxi and give him a towel. I said I would drive him, but he refused. He said I must not be anywhere near him. It hurt me horribly, but I didn't realize what he was doing yet. He went to the airport and flew to Minneapolis."

"What?"

"It was the next plane out, I guess. He went to the hospital immediately but had lost too much blood. To save me from manslaughter charges, he died in a strange town, with no one nearby to hold his hand and see him past the pearly gates. It was the darkest day yet in my life. Since then, I have only once had a worse day."

"When was that?"

"A week ago."

✲ 48 ✲

ON THE BALCONY

Back in the hotel room, we showered and drip-dried our naked bodies on the balcony. We were high up, but I bet a few Paulistas got an eyeful. The weather was warm and muggy. There were incredible trees everywhere with bright yellow, red, and purple blossoms. Oklahoma is so different. The whole place dried up and blew away just thirty years ago, and if it weren't for oil, it would be empty now. There are no pretty trees or giant fruit plates back home.

"Cody, you heard the bad news, right?"

"Not sure I understood it."

"Well, I can suck you, you can suck me, I can fuck you, but you can't fuck me for at least another week, and only if it doesn't hurt too much."

Cody laughed.

"I think we'll manage. Did you ask him if I can eat your ass?"

"Uh, no. He was a doctor."

Cody folded his arms and growled, "Brightie, I'm disappointed in you."

I grinned at him, and he chuckled. "I shouldn't joke, sorry. I'm going to eat your ass right now."

Out on the balcony, he kneeled and licked my anus. I grabbed the railing to keep my knees from buckling.

It sent waves of pleasure in all directions. I closed my eyes and saw the waves, like sunbeams, warming my body.

"You like it?" Cody asked.

"Mmm hmm." I was too worked up to talk. My cock stood tall. Cody reached up and held onto it like a balloon at the carnival. He stroked it back and forth until pre-cum dribbled out. He stuck his head between my legs and turned to catch the first drops.

Holding me by the waist and cock, with his head buried in my ass, he brought me inside to the big bed with a purple quilt. My knees automatically went to my ears. I forgot Cody couldn't enter yet. I wrapped them around his neck while he licked and stroked me until I was just a trickling stream of dick juice. Cody took breaks from sucking my ass to lick the pre-cum from his fat fingers.

He rotated me so my head was dangling off the edge of the bed. I knew what came next. Not as good as the butt, but at least he's inside me. He put the small soft head of his cock in my mouth. I watched it balloon up to its full size as his hardening cock forced the head to the back of my throat and past my tonsils into the food tube. And it was food for me. I sucked, gulped, gagged, and did everything I could to let Cody know how important it was to me.

I could see only Cody's thick legs and giant balls, so I was surprised when I felt hands on my waist. Cody lifted me off the bed, turned me upside down, and put my dick in his mouth. He pressed my bottom, forcing me forward until I reached his tonsils, then went beyond. Upside down, my arms wrapped around his waist and his around mine, he walked us back out onto the balcony. The mild breeze blew on my wet butthole. I wanted Cody to put a finger or two in there, but it was off-limits. To be so close to what you want and not be allowed to have it is so terrible that it can almost feel good. Besides, I like putting my dick in Cody's butt. I can do that.

I forgot to breathe. Upside down, the need for air comes very suddenly. I pushed on Cody's thighs and managed to pop his giant head back past my airway into my mouth. I took several deep but soft breaths, then let go of his thighs, letting his huge cock rush down my throat again. I squeezed the sides of my throat to feel him sliding in and out. Cody rocked his big ass back and forth to fuck my face. Suspended like I was, I had a harder time thrusting and didn't want to finish here anyway. I took his balls and rubbed them on my cheek. Then I put a finger to my mouth and tested Cody's cock. It was covered in thick spit from deep in my throat. I rubbed two fingers in the saliva before I let the monster return to its cave deep in my throat.

I took those two slippery fingers and worked them into Cody's furry butthole. He didn't need any coaching now. He set me down on the bed. He took my spit-slick cock out of his mouth. He found a tiny bottle of hotel lotion to grease up his ass.

Staring at those mountains of flesh with the puckered hole in the center, I wondered how I ever thought I should be the only one to take it all inside me. It was like Cody's story - it feels so good to let go of all the manly responsibility and let someone else make a woman of you. It's the most relaxing sensation to have a huge cock sliding inside you, rubbing against you, waiting for it to fill you with cum. And when the cock is attached to a huge hunk of a man like Cody, it's multiplied seven times over.

But it was my turn to let Cody be the woman. He could forget his giant cock and let my big dick do some work. He could gaze at the flowery light fixture and count the number of petals. He could draw circles around my nipples and then squeeze them to make me come. He deserved to have that, too.

I would make him my wife tonight. I stood over him, his face down on the purple bedspread, his ass right at the perfect height for me to enter.

Holding him at the hips, I pressed my spit-covered cock against his tight ass. Cody wriggled. I slapped his butt and saw the hole open just slightly. Another slap, and this time I was ready for it; I forced my thick cock head into him. I wanted to be gentle, but I knew this was a situation where a little cruelty up front was much kinder. The thickest part of my meat, the ring at the bottom of the head, made a popping noise when it snapped past the big bull rider's sphincter. Cody made no sound. He was screaming like a little girl inside, no doubt, but he was too tough to yield to pain. That was the worst of it. To show how I would like him to be with me, I waited patiently until the spasms of pain ended. Forcing my way in while those waves were trying to force me out was painful and unnecessary.

I made it my goal to give Cody all the pleasure I had to offer. I moved through the anus, but when I reached the inner sphincter, I didn't force my way past. I just pushed softly, and it gave. As I slid my long, thick cock through that tight hole, Cody turned his head to me. His eyes were fluttering. His body was trembling.

"Oh god, how are you doing that?"

"Gently."

I found the spot the Brazilian doctor's chart called the rectal valve. I tickled it back and forth with my cock head, driving Cody wild. He pounded the bed.

"Yes! Yes! Don't stop, Brightie." Cody didn't command or whine; he just asked.

That valve was a ridge of skin that rubbed just right against my cockhead. Rubbing it brought me close to coming, and I wasn't all the way in. To see Cody enjoying the touch of my dick inside him made me dizzy. I didn't want to come because I was only a little more than halfway, but my body had other ideas. My balls pulled up, and then the orgasm began. At the same time, Cody's trembling increased. His ass cheeks were jiggling against the exposed part of my penis. I shot a bunch of come at the back of the rectum. I pushed in deeper; the semen flooded Cody's sigmoid colon.

"Don't stop, Brightie. Come in me again. Deeper." Again, just an easy request, nothing hysterical or angry about it. I expected my cock to grow soft before being forced out of Cody's ass, but it didn't. Cody's uncontrollable quivering made his fat butt cheeks massage the base of my long, thick dick. It made me harder and bigger, not softer. I pushed up and over the wall into the colon.

At last, my pubic hairs were tickling Cody's butthole, and my balls were touching his. Then I edged back out of the colon, crept back over the wall, sent Cody to the moon as I dragged past the rectal valve, and popped out of the rectum into the anus. Slowly, I reversed directions and went deeper.

The slow pace was driving Cody wild. He beat the mattress, bellowed, groaned, and growled. He enjoyed every inch of my cock. I kept on giving Cody a silent anatomy lesson. I had studied those charts on the doctor's wall, and I knew where everything was. I knew that when I stuffed inside him fully, the base of my cock narrowed. The most pleasure Cody felt was when my cock was in his anus at the thickest point, pressing hard against the prostate gland. I spent a lot of time with the widest part of my dick sliding in and out of the anus. When I slowed down, it was even better. Cody's dick was hanging off the bed, resting below my shin. As I moved that fat part of my cock back and forth over the prostate, it was like milking a cow. Spoonfuls of precum ran down my shin to the ankle.

"Yes. Yes. Yes." Cody whispered.

For variety, I would pound in all the way and hold it there, then remove my entire cock in a sudden movement. Cody's butthole would remain stretched, like a cave, waiting for my cock to light a fire for the night. The first time I pulled out, a trickle of semen came with me. I expected there to be more. I knew I needed to come again.

To bring myself closer, I rubbed my dick head on all the bumps and ridges. The transition between the rectum and the colon was the best. It was so slippery. I wondered what could make it so slick; then I remembered how all my semen pushed itself in there. It created a lotion more perfect than Albolene or Oura.

I rubbed against the first segment of the colon; it made me proud. The doctor said that less than 1% of men can reach the wall, let alone pass into the colon. I was abnormal like Cody. Not as much, but abnormal. It felt good to be different; so good, the tingling started.

The tingling must be a magnet or an electrical pulse because Cody became tingly, too. He pinched my nipple with one hand. He used his other hand to tweak his own. My balls gurgled. My dick grew impossibly thick, stretching Cody even further. Before that first splash could make its way out the tip, I removed myself entirely. Cody was a giant gaping hole now. I shot part of my load into his wide-open ass, then shoved myself quickly inside. I went deep, past the wall, and finished coming in his colon.

"Brightie, holy shit, you're good." Cody was stroking himself like a sinner. I pushed him, so he did a somersault onto the bed, his huge cock pointing right at me. I leaned, took the head into my mouth, and then swallowed it deep in my throat. I found a spot where I wanted to throw up, but if I didn't, my throat would tighten around Cody. I stayed there, retching silently, until Cody let loose a massive injection of sperm straight into my tummy. I counted fourteen squirts in all. I cleaned him up on the way out. My whole mouth and throat tingled with the flavor of Cody's cum.

Cody motioned me over. He was kneeling, holding a glass tumbler etched with the hotel name. With a loud fart, he spewed my cum into the glass. He farted three more times, each one bigger than the last. A silent fifth fart produced one last dribble.

We stared at the glass. It was the kind you use for orange juice and was half full.

"Here, Brightie, you made it; you should have it."

"That's not how it works, Cody. I already had a huge helping of yours. The way I see it, that's all yours."

It gave off steam like a fresh bowl of grits. Cody downed it and kissed me, sharing the last drops. It tasted better mixed with Cody's sweet mouth. It tasted like grits with butter.

❦ 49 ❦

JESSE AND FRANK

The flight home went a different path. We flew to Caracas, then Miami. The connecting flight to Houston was the next day, so we booked a hotel in Miami Beach to pass the time. We couldn't leave the airport in Caracas, so we waited in the first-class lounge. While I was there, I thought I should have a shower and change my clothes. When putting on my shirt, I found two lumps in the pocket. I took out the Brazilian flags that Joao and Paulo had given me. The thick flagpoles each had a gold finial. I discovered I could unscrew it. Inside each hollow pole was a cigarette. It didn't smell like tobacco. It must be marijuana. Cody appeared wrapped in a big white bath towel. He saw my surprise package and laughed. His laughter attracted a couple of businessmen who wanted in on the joke. He pointed to my tattered flags and explained.

We all had a good laugh. These guys were Venezuelan salesmen, but they worked in the Miami office of their company. They told me that here in the airport, marijuana was legal, but anywhere else in Venezuela, I could expect a long jail sentence. We decided it would be best if the four of us smoked it before flying to the US, where policies were even stricter.

I took a good look at the men. They wore the typical black business suits with white shirts and colorful ties. The taller one had wavy brown hair and brown eyes. He was named Francisco; In the States, he was Frank. The shorter one had black hair and blue eyes. He was named Jesus but went by Jesse. Frank had a lighter. We all crowded into a changing room and lit the cigarette.

I smoked cigarettes with Bill Gresham but never marijuana. Cody warned me, but I didn't listen. I took a long drag and immediately coughed. Even in the short time that the smoke was in my lungs, it had an effect. My mind got hazy the same way the room got smoky. As the first cigarette made the rounds, I watched the men hold a small amount in their lungs for a long time. I was still coughing when they handed it back to me. I took a small drag and held it. After a few seconds, I had to cough again. But this time, it was just the one cough, and I was fine.

I surveyed the room. Cody flexed his wing muscles as he lifted the cigarette to his lips. His arm curled, and his bicep grew. Everything about Cody grew, I realized. He was like a big god trying to escape from a little human body. I needed to tell him this at that very instant.

"Cody, you're big, but keep getting so much bigger." He turned to me and smiled. "Are you just a man? Or are you a god, Cody?"

Frank laughed. "Man, what are you saying?"

"Cody has these soft muscles," I pinched his relaxed bicep and wings. "But then they become enormous." I prompted Cody to lift and flex. "Do you see?"

The two men stared. It was my turn for another puff. Holding it in, I handed Cody what was left of the cigarette and watched in awe as his muscles rippled with every movement. It was as ⬤ had never seen him before. I took off my shirt and looked at my own body. It was puny by comparison.

I nodded at Frank and Jesse. They removed their coats, ties, button-down shirts, and undershirts. Frank was lanky and hairless, like me. Jesse was short and barrel-chested, with big hairy arms and silver-dollar-sized tits. Both men had creamy white skin that glowed under the lamplight. The second cigarette was making its way around the room. Nobody spoke. I was high on marihuana, so I didn't know if it was my imagination or real, but there was this vibe like sex was about to start. I didn't break the silence in case I was wrong.

I tried to see where I sat cross-legged on the floor. The ground was ten feet below me. I struggled to return to the floor but couldn't. When I looked up, Frank and Jesse were kissing. I think.

Cody sat in a chair, his penis hidden in the folds of the towel. It was a low chair, and I wondered if his cockhead was touching the floor. That might be how I could come down. I put my hand under his towel and had no trouble finding his soft meat swinging below his knees. His dick wasn't touching the ground, but his feet were. I saw them now, and it was like I saw them for the first time. I studied how big and beautiful they were. He kept his toenails trimmed. I licked his big toe and put it in my mouth. Every toe needed my attention. I licked each one in turn and cleaned it in my mouth. Cody's towel was rising. I remembered we had company. Frank and Jesse were undoing each other's belts. The marijuana was all gone.

When Frank's pants dropped, a long thin erection popped out. Jesse bent to take it in his mouth, pulling his pants down as well. From my angle, licking the soles of Cody's foot, I only saw Jesse's hairy butt. It was shaped like two cantaloupes. Frank tapped Jesse and pointed. Cody was getting close to full mast, and it broke through the gap in the towel. Jesse made the sign of the cross. Both men stopped completely. When Jesse turned, he was hard. His penis was average length, but it was big around as a jar of Derby tamales. He was thicker than Cody.

It was me who started it all. I wanted to hold Jesse's tamale jar, so I just reached over and put both hands on it. My thumbs and forefingers couldn't quite touch.

"You like that?" He asked as he kissed me. His mouth was soft like cotton candy. I didn't have to answer; my dick drooled on his leg. I rubbed my hands up and down the massive stump of cock. I knew I had won when Jesse dribbled too. He stared at my long, thick dick with envy and desire.

"You want to fuck me, Brightie? Cuz I can't fuck nobody." It was a familiar sadness. I studied his enormous cock. It needed to go into someone's hole. Cody couldn't do it, but I knew I could - except for the doctor's orders. But those were orders for Cody. Jesse wouldn't ever reach the back where all the troubles were. I could do it.

I glanced over my shoulder and saw Frank taking a few inches of Cody into his mouth. I realized he must get a lot of practice with Jesse. Cody was training him on how to take him deep. It was going well.

I winked at Jesse. He was expecting rejection. I surprised him. "Do you see that?" I pointed to Frank swallowing Cody. "He fucks me all the time. I'm a professional."

Jesse brightened. "Can I fuck you?"

I reached into my toiletry bag and took out a tube of Albolene. "Be my guest."

Cody glared at me. I held my hands up wide and moved them closer, out of view from Jesse, who was coating his tamale can with lotion. Cody frowned, shook his head, paused, then shrugged. I had his blessing.

Marijuana heightened every sensation, and the pain

was one of them. Jesse waited at the back door until I opened it for him. He shoved a little too hard, and the short fat head of his dick popped in. I saw colors in the air. Then I smelled Jesse's manly sweat. It was like amyl nitrite for me. I buried my nose in his armpit, and my anus welcomed him in. It was strange to have someone so thick fucking me in the front of my butthole, never even reaching the middle valve. What felt great was his extreme thickness pressing up hard against my prostate. I oozed and flowed, soaking my belly in my own pre-cum. The smile on Jesse's face made me feel like a hero. I was high, but that smile was not an exaggerated sensation.

"Thank you." It came out as a whisper.

"Any time," I answered. It was an empty invitation - I doubted we would ever see one another again. He was still hammering his short, obese cock into my hole. I was stretched beyond the limits of human flesh. Then I realized I might be a god as well, stretching to receive prayers in the form of semen. My mind would clear up; then it would float back into the hazy smoke that filled the room. My kisses with Jesse became passionate. I held my hands on his hard, round, furry ass and pushed him into me, harder, deeper. At the same time, his tongue found my mouth and filled it. He tasted like scotch and cigars. His legs were thick with muscle. He put great power into every thrust.

Jesse was fucking me hard. In his enthusiasm, he pulled too far and fell out. I could feel the ceiling fan blowing on the inside of my anus. Jesse's eyes opened wide. I was his first fuck in a long time, maybe ever, and my abilities excited him.

He moved me so I could see my ass in the changing room mirror. He fucked me hard and deep and pulled out. My ass was a huge dark hole, several inches across. It closed quickly, but I wanted to see it. I gripped the sides and pulled, stretching myself even wider. I had a lot of sex in the past month, but I had never seen an ass like mine. Holding it wide as I did, Jesse could insert himself without touching the sides. I let it go, and it snapped tight against his thickness. "Oh shit." he moaned.

I brushed a nipple with the back of my hand, and he shuddered. I pinched it, and he grabbed my wrist. I locked eyes with him. He shook his head. "It's too sensitive." It was hard to believe a fireplug like Jesse was sensitive, but I stopped.

Jesse's thrusts had milked my prostate gland dry. I felt a strange, warming sensation in my butt. With each thrust, the ridges in my anus began tingling. The drugs may have helped, but Jesse's fat dick caused a massive seizure in my butt. It was like shooting a load, but it was my butt, not my dick, that was throbbing. Unlike a regular orgasm, where the pleasure peaks and then subsides completely, this anal orgasm was an ever-growing wave of ecstasy. I had no choice but to cry out.

"Oh. Gaaaah. Unh. Oh fuck Jesse, oh fuck. Oh god, I'm coming in there. I'm coming in there. You're making me come. My lower body shook like a rag doll. Cody popped up like a prairie dog, concerned, but when he saw my face, he smiled and returned to his lesson on deep-throat fucking with Frank.

I expected the anal throbbing to subside, but it only ebbed. Each time it came back, it was more intense. Jesse's extreme girth stretched me in every direction. His hard thrusts caused the orgasms to grow bigger and bigger. I wondered if it was possible to die from pleasure. Every square inch of my rectum was throbbing in response to the constant thrusting and stretching. It was my out-of-control bucking that sent Jesse past the fence. He grunted, and the sweat on his neck and forehead came down in a heavy rain. It smelled so good it sent me into another intense set of spasms. I licked the sweat from his armpit. It tasted like turkey gravy and underwear.

I was on the brink of an orgasm, the regular kind where you ejaculate. I licked the edge of Jesse's left tit. He didn't protest. A soft tongue was better than pinching fingers. I knew it was happening because he closed his eyes and let his head drop back.

"Oh yes! Oh goddamn! Brightie! Oh, you hot fucking clown. You're making me; you're gonna make me, you—"

Jesse released air from his lungs as his fat pecker throbbed upward, pressing hard against my prostate gland. His sperm spewed inside me. It was warm and slippery. It was enough to cause me to orgasm in my butt and my dick at the same time. Never in my life had I experienced anything like it. Every part of my body felt like the head of my penis. As Jesse thrust, I moaned. When his arm brushed against mine, I shuddered the same as if he had stroked my dick head. Just as the first ropes of cum began to spurt out of me, Jesse moved his leg, and I saw in the mirror his tamale can dick stretching me past the limit. Jesse's cock popped out and landed on his thigh with a loud smack. I stared again at my wide-open hole in the mirror. It excited me so much; I think I may have started to come a second time before I was done with the first. Spurt after spurt of cum came flying out of me. When I could see my gaping ass close, my body gave off several farts that pushed out Jesse's cum. Because of the anal orgasm, and maybe because I had smoked too much marijuana, I believed that my anus was coming at the same time as my penis.

I quaked a few more times before the internal orgasms stopped. I stroked Jesse's handsome, smiling face. He caressed my cheek. "Was I any good?"

I laughed. "You're a natural, Jesse. I had an orgasm everywhere. Your fat cock is a magic wand."

"Pretty short for a wand, don't you think?" He was putting himself down. I couldn't let him walk away thinking he was inadequate.

I whispered into Jesse's ear. "I've done it with Cody dozens of times, and I never once had anything like that with him."

"Yeah, but I'll bet he goes a lot deeper."

"He does. But he doesn't cause my ass to go into orgasm. He's not as thick as you. You have a talent. Don't waste it."

I followed Jesse's gaze to where Cody was nearing his climax with Frank.

Jesse went all teary-eyed. "Frank won't let me."

Cody tightened his butt cheeks and squeezed his eyes shut hard. Frank was not enjoying having Cody gagging him and blocking his airway. Tears poured out of his eyes. He had the drive to finish what he started. Cody's thighs shook as he released his load into his throat. Frank swallowed it hungrily, then retreated so Cody was only in his mouth. Jesse's eyes widened as he saw the length of flesh that came out of his friend's throat. Whenever I see Cody's immense log of flesh, I am impressed, so I know what must be going through Jesse's head.

"Jesse, if Frank can take Cody down his throat, he can take you up his ass."

"He refuses."

"Play along with me," I whispered.

I spoke in a tone that was just loud enough for Frank to hear while he regained his breath. "Jesse, does Frank have anal orgasms when you guys do it?"

Jesse shook his head.

"Why not? I doubt any man could take a fucking from you and not start shaking like I did. Not even Cody does that."

Jesse picked up on what I was doing. "Um, most guys don't let me."

"Well, you're lucky you have Frank. I give Cody my ass all the time. It stopped hurting the very first time, and now it's always easy."

Jesse shrugged. "Yeah, Frank doesn't know how lucky he is."

I shot a glance over at Jesse's unwilling partner and saw the facial expression I expected. Things were going to change for these two.

❧ 50 ❧

MIAMI

J esse and Frank flew economy, so we didn't see them again until we reached the baggage claim area at Miami International. Winking at me, Jesse brushed his palm across Frank's ass. Frank jumped, but he smiled. In about half an hour, our luggage showed up.

Frank asked, "Where are you guys staying?"

"The Fontainebleau," Cody answered.

Jesse whistled. "We got us a millionaire here."

Cody did his best impersonation of a comfortable laugh.

Frank said, "If you don't already have a limo, we'd be happy to give you a ride. We rent an apartment in Miami Beach."

Cody and I sat in the back of the massive Plymouth convertible. The top was down, and the sun shone at a different angle than back home. It was humid like a thunderstorm would pop up at any minute. I watched Jesse drive in the front seat while Frank leaned his head against his shoulder. I did one better and lay on my back, watching the palm trees whiz by, my head in Cody's lap. There were stirrings in his groin. I gave out a sigh of frustration. We still had a few days before I could let him deep inside. He adjusted himself and ran his fingers through my hair. I reached up and played with his nipple once I found it poking out underneath the cowboy shirt. It was a magic button. On Cody's instant hardon, my head rose two inches above Cody's lap. Cody wasn't mad, but he sure was frustrated like me.

The two salesmen accepted our invitation to join us for a drink. I had stayed at a few nice hotels since I met Cody, but none could hold a candle to this one. It was a huge glass and concrete semicircle. It reminded me of Guilherme's house if it were stacked ten high and twenty long.

Inside, everything was modern and new. The tiled black and white floors and the stone columns were arranged in patterns that I had never seen in nature. The bar sat under a giant stone made from concrete and carnival glass. The stores didn't sell shampoo; they sold clothing that cost thousands of dollars. Dressed as a cowboy, I thought they would run me out. Instead, all these old rich people turned and smiled. One old lady tugged my sleeve and asked, "Are you a real cowboy?"

"I'm in the rodeo."

"Oh, that's the real thing. You make America a better place. Keep at it!"

I smiled and blushed. It was the most rich people I had been around at one time.

We started off with beers and ended with J&B. Jesse and Frank were too drunk to drive, so they came to our room.

The room was huge, with an ocean view through floor-to-ceiling glass windows. Below, there was a swimming pool in the shape of a cat. You could only tell from above.

I turned back and fought off a surge of jealousy as Cody kissed both men, holding them in his strong arms. He motioned me over, and we all took turns kissing one another. It was hot. Soon I could see the fabric throb over Cody's trapped cock. Frank tented out his checkerboard shorts, and Jesse stretched the seams of his zipper.

Frank broke the silence. "Cody, how do you fuck him?"

Cody was tipsy. "Ask Brightie. He does all the work."

Frank turned to me. "You took my, uh, friend in the ass today. How?"

I looked at Jesse. He grinned. "On my back."

Frank smiled. "No, silly; I mean, how do you take something that big into something this small?"

"There's a couple of tricks to it. First, you gotta accept that it's gonna hurt like a motherfucker at first, okay?"

Frank nodded, taking mental notes.

"Uh, I fight bulls for a living, so pain isn't a big deal for me like it is for most people. So once you accept pain as part of the whole thing, you do the most painful thing first."

"What's that?" Frank was interested. Even Cody and Jesse leaned in for my lesson.

"It depends on the shape of the cock. In most cases, I think it's popping the head past your hole. The head is usually the biggest part."

Nods of agreement encouraged me to continue.

"Make sure you use good lotion. The wrong kind will burn or cause a lot of friction. Cody uses Albolene. Now I do, too."

To prove it, Cody took a big tub of Albolene out of his overnight bag.

"Another secret - spit and Albolene don't mix, which means spit makes it better."

"I don't get you." Jesse was intrigued.

"I mean, the spit is slippery, and so is the Albolene, and since they can't mix, they each slide off the other. So it's like double slippery."

"What else? Oh yeah, when it starts to hurt, the

best thing to do is to push like you're trying to poop. It helps a lot."

Cody held up a disposable enema. "Don't forget these."

"Oh, right. I use one every day, sometimes twice a day, so that I can be ready. You gotta clean down there."

Cody tossed one to Frank and one to me.

"Show him how it's done, Cody."

It was awkward, but the bathroom was so nice I didn't care.

"You don't need to clean like I do. A fuck from Cody requires a deep cleaning. So for you, you're going to go like this." I squatted over the throne-like toilet and inserted the enema tip.

"Put it in all the way. Then give a slow, steady squeeze. Keep it tight so the water stays in."

I filled my rectum with the cool water and set the enema on the counter.

"Hold it for as long as you can, but not more than a minute."

"Should I hop up and down?" Frank was serious.

"No. Just stay on the toilet until you're ready. I drape my dick over the toilet seat so it doesn't catch any spray."

And I released a clear stream of water. Some of Jesse's come floated to the top. I was clean as a whistle.

"Now, your turn. It may be a little messy. I was already clean."

Frank did as he was told. The bathroom filled with a stench when he let go. Frank was embarrassed.

"Let's fill yours up again."

I unscrewed the cap and refilled the plastic bottle. We kept at it until he was as clean as me.

We came out of the bathroom naked from the waist down. Cody was kissing Jesse. It was comical - Jesse's dick looked like Cody's if someone had cut it off. Jesse tugged on Cody, who grunted approval.

I kissed Frank until our cocks were at full attention. I wasn't done with the lesson, so I cleared my throat.

"For Frank to become an expert, he needs a team to coach him."

Cody tilted his head, "What did you have in mind?"

"I think the best thing is for Jesse to fuck Frank while Cody fucks me."

"But—" Cody protested, but I held up a finger.

"It should be an accurate simulation, so he should only go six inches deep at most." The thought of Cody only partway inside me, pressing that huge cockhead against my prostate was enough to cause a bead of pre-cum to drip from my cock.

A few minutes later, I was on the bed beside Frank, holding his hand. Cody and Jesse had switched off a few times while licking and spitting in our butts. Jesse wanted me again, but I couldn't do that to Frank.

The top portion of Cody's cock glistened with Albolene, and Frank was thoroughly coated.

It was turning into a horse race.

"Place the head at the hole. It's closed. Press gently at first, then harder until the hole gives. When it opens, do not stop until the whole head of your cock is in. Frank, I found this. Break it and inhale it right when your body lets him in." I handed him a vial of amyl nitrite.

"On your marks, get set, go!"

Cody was so familiar to me; I would have let him in immediately. I wanted to stay in tune with Frank, so I stayed clamped shut until I saw him lift the vial to his nose. Cody and Jesse pushed in until their heads were all the way inside us.

I sighed with familiarity. Frank came out of the amyl haze and made horrible cries of pain. I pushed the amyl back to his nose. "Jesse, stay in there, no matter what."

Frank tore at the bedsheets and thrashed. I held his

hand. I kissed him and promised him it would get better very quickly.

Cody beamed with pride that I was such a good teacher.

In a short while, Frank's grip on my hand loosened.

"Jesse, can you force a little more blood, you know, to make your cock swell for a second or two?"

"Like this?" He squeezed his butt cheeks together to force more blood into his tamale jar.

Frank moaned. It wasn't pain. He loved the stretch.

"Yeah, keep doing that for a minute."

Cody did the same with me. His pulses were slow because of the length the blood had to travel, but they worked. I moaned like a winter wind when I felt my hole stretch more.

I could barely speak. "Frank, do you like that?"

His eyes blazed with desire when he nodded.

"That's just a small taste of what Jesse can give you every day, three times a day if you want it."

Jesse held up his arms and flexed his biceps. Frank reached over and squeezed my hand.

I took charge of step two. "Okay, this part shouldn't hurt, but just in case, let's both take a whiff of amyl just before. Cody, Jesse, when I say go, I want you to go the full six inches. You should pass through a couple of tight areas."

I took a long whiff after Frank, and we both laid back with our heads throbbing. Cody got too enthusiastic and pushed too far. I used a foot on his thigh to push and reposition him. It didn't hurt, but I didn't think it was fair.

"Okay, Frank, how are we doing?" When I turned for an answer, I saw Frank's eyes fluttering. Jesse was going full throttle. I guess my lesson ended early.

The bed shook over and over again as Jesse gave his sex buddy the first of many anal orgasms. Fred's cries of pleasure were music to my ears.

Cody was doing a frightened dance in my anus. He was afraid to hurt me. I brought him close and whispered. "You don't have to be careful until you're another mile deeper. Go crazy."

Cody fucked the first six inches of my rectum with renewed vigor. He held his cock at the eight-inch mark to prevent any deep thrusts.

It was disappointing to have Cody inside me, but only a little way. That is, until the miracle happened. With Jesse, the anal throbbing was a slow buildup. I didn't know him, his thickness was different, and I didn't have a strong connection with him. With Cody, it was like I got jumped. We had never done this kind of sex, where his head, the thickest part, was down where all the nerves were. I rubbed the muscles on his tummy and stared into his eyes. Then my mouth flew open, and I took a sudden deep breath.

"What did I hurt you?" Cody tried to pull out, but I grabbed his hand at the eight-inch mark and forced him to stay. I shook my head.

"It feels good?" I couldn't speak, only nod.

With Frank wiggling and jiggling next to me, the shockwaves continued. These were ten times stronger than what Jesse did to me this morning. I had to stay silent because any word coming out would have been a holler. My neck turned side to side; my chest tightened and loosened. My waist rocked up and down. My fists clenched and unclenched. My thighs tightened, and my toes curled. None of it was me. I mean, I didn't do it; my body did it to me. Cody was fucking fast and hard but shallow, dragging his head across my prostate over and over. My penis covered my belly with pre-come. Cody put a fat index finger where the sticky dribbles ran into my belly button and licked it like a popsicle.

Cody leaned over and put the top half of my dick in his mouth. Jesse saw and did the same but couldn't reach Frank's without popping out. Instead, Jesse began stroking Frank's long, thin cock. Frank was too far gone at this point. He couldn't speak. And I knew just how he felt.

The room became a gallery of strange noises. Grunts and "Aw yeahs" from our men on top; moans, whines, and whimpers from the two of us on our backs. The bed creaked and groaned. I was afraid it might break under the strain of all the thrashing, twitching, and bucking of our anal orgasms.

Cody was worried. I didn't know how to reassure him. My hand was still on his clenched fist. I rubbed it softly with my thumb. Now Cody's eyes fluttered. My little thumb on his giant fist got to him; that made me even more aroused. Any time my pleasure increased with his, it turned me on even more. That's how you end up coming.

I stroked his hairy fist. I put my other hand on the big piece of his cock still outside me. When I tickled the skin, Cody stumbled. I found another weak spot for me to use. Tickling his cock and fist combined was such a tiny movement, but it caused a colossal explosion. Cody's legs buckled. He let my cock fall from his mouth.

"Oh fuck, Brightie, how are you doing that to me? I'm gonna; you're making me. Unhhh." The semen filled the upper part of my rectum and kept coming. The pressure as Cody unplugged my hole pushed against my prostate, and this time, instead of pre-cum, my cock came for real. It was like the oil geysers in Sturgis. I heard drops fall all around me. Cody had my cum on his legs, in his mustache, and on his left tit. Even Jesse and Frank got splattered. I put both hands on my head and pulled the skin tight across my face. I don't know why; it just felt good. Then Cody's cum erupted from my asshole. It stained the bed and Cody's boots.

Frank was about to erupt himself. I went back into coaching mode.

"Jesse, make sure you come first." He focused on giving Frank the first good fuck of his life.

I whispered in Frank's ear, "If you want to make him come, lick his titty."

Frank shook his head. "I don't ever want it to end."

But the two hairy cantaloupes of Jesse's muscled ass thrust harder, harder, then stopped. With a quiet shout, Jesse delivered a helping of hot sperm up Frank's butt. Jesse then gave small short thrusts right over the prostate while rubbing his hand on his friend's penis. Frank was already leaking cum out of his loosened asshole when he shot his load. It went very high. I think it might have hit the chandelier.

❧ 51 ❧

GET BACK ON THE HORSE

Frank and Jesse stayed the night. In the morning, Frank could barely walk.

"I'm holding you accountable, Brightie." He pointed at me. "I'm permanently damaged."

I laughed. Jesse gave me a dirty look.

"This is the worst it will get. Once you start today, it will be fine."

Frank was crazy mad. "There is no way he's going to put that— thing — in me again!"

The frown on Jesse's face was so sad, it hurt.

"The lesson ain't over yet." I should have explained it before we started.

"Frank, maybe we should just leave." Jesse was wiping away tears.

"No! Please hear me out."

Frank folded his arms. "I'd sit down, but..." He laughed at his own joke. I smiled.

"Okay, the day after Cody first fucked me, I was in a world of pain. But he wanted more. I know this will sound strange, but the second time cured the first. And after the third time, there's no pain once he's inside you."

Frank and Jesse doubted me.

"I know it's hard to believe, but you gotta trust me."

Cody stepped forward. "The boy is telling the truth."

Frank gaped at me. "You mean I can have sex again today, and it will be good?"

"Yup, after the first bit."

Cody said, "A friend told me the same after my first good fuck, and it was true. You have maybe one more day of pain and a lifetime of pleasure ahead of you."

"But you gotta hop back on the horse and keep riding," I added.

Frank smiled and asked, "Does it have to be such a wide saddle?"

❧ 52 ❧
HOME

That evening, we pulled into Cody's place in McKinney. I had forgotten how beautiful the house was. Now that I knew where his money came from and how much he had lost to get it, the beauty was mixed with sadness. Cody's staff set up a guest room for me, but I didn't want it. Over dinner, he told me I had to stay there so he wouldn't be tempted. Dinner was fried tacos and black beans. It wasn't appetizing to look at, but it was delicious. I had never even heard of black beans. They tasted even better with sour cream on top.

I wasn't happy sleeping in the guest room. Maybe Cody was right; maybe we did need alone time. I kicked back in bed and remembered all the crazy things we had done. I thought about that bath house in Peru and Guilherme's modern mansion. I remembered Cody turning vicious for no reason. I was still nervous he might change back. I knew he did those things because he was so afraid of losing me. The door opened; it was Cody.

"Sorry, Brightie, I couldn't wait to share the news." He held a stack of letters in his hand.

I never miss an opportunity. "Come sit here and show me." I patted the giant bed.

Cody just sat his big ass on the bed and didn't even notice what I was up to. "Look here, Brightie. The Brazilian Rodeo Association published an article about you and me, and that show we did. I haven't seen it, but all the other associations seem to have. Get a load of all these letters! We have our pick of destinations. There's California, New York City, London, Mexico City, Buenos Aires, Tokyo, and Hong Kong!"

"Can we do all of them?"

"Well, a few dates overlap, but yeah, we could be traveling all next year. You're gonna have to move in with me, though."

"Why?"

"Clinton doesn't have an airport. And I need to be sure you get enough sex."

I laughed. "That we get enough sex, you mean?"

Cody blushed and rubbed his pant leg like a naughty child.

I made my next move. I hugged him and kissed his cheek. I stared at his handsome face. "Thank you for changing my whole life, Cody. I'm just a farm boy from Oklahoma, and you made me a star."

Cody held me close the way a dad might do. "You are so much more than a farm boy, Brightie."

I only had to look at the growing bulge in his pant leg to know what was coming. He smashed his lips into mine. I smiled even as we kissed and stripped off our clothes.

AFTERWORD BY THE AUTHOR

The rough and tumble world of the rodeo cowboy is rarely so tolerant of deviancy as it is depicted here. This book is a fantasy I wrote, dreaming of a world where love between men was neither criminal (such as in Brazil, where it's legal) nor treated as an illness. The love between men is real, the sex is beautiful, and it happens all around the world—that part I did not make up. Cody has a huge problem many men think they want. They might think again if they knew what kind of isolation and loneliness Cody has experienced. I hope this book has demonstrated the pain of being abnormal. The cure for abnormality? I sent in a clown. Brightie is the perfect match for Cody. He's imaginary and far too beautiful to be true. But he's a wonderful clown who fights off bulls and entertains big crowds. That a clown can enjoy the love of other men, that is true. Our world is too coarse to understand the love between men. It is as lasting as love between a man and a woman. Without marriage, there is an even stronger bond forged between lonesome cowboys. I believe Cody and Brightie will live the rest of their lives together; their bond is so perfect it requires no contract.

—Peter Schutes, Santa Monica, CA 1961

ABOUT PETER SCHUTES

Peter Schutes is a fictional character. He was modeled after the gay pulp fiction authors of the 1970s and 1980s. His creator often wondered who the men were who wrote these books, and so he created Peter to satisfy his curiosity.

Peter was born in 1896 to a wealthy New England family. His whole life, he carried a massive burden: he had a gigantic penis. His sex life was defined by the men who worshipped him.

Peter led a tempestuous life, which is documented in the fictional masterpiece "The Autobiography of Peter Schutes." To learn more about this prolific and prodigious author, we recommend reading his immortal tale of life with too much of a good thing.

OTHER BOOKS FROM PETER SCHUTES PUBLISHING

E-books and Paperbacks (as noted)

The Able Seaman

The Anaconda Copper

The Autobiography of Peter Schutes*

Backwoods Delivery

Big Bodies of All Sizes*

Big Hole River*

Bobbing Buoys and Salty Seamen*

Bunkhouse Buddies*

The Butt Baby*

Cloistered

Dark as a Dungeon*

Demonic Deception *aka* Deceived, Cursed & Blessed

Desert Island Daddies

The Expectant Member

Firehouse Lovers

The Fish

Five Erotic Tales*

The Gospel of Priapus*

Hercules and Lippos

Hobo Honey

Hot Blue Collars*

Hotshot

Logger's Delight

Muscle Bottom*

Panama Heat

Satanic Seductions*

Satan's Sissy Boy

The Slaves of Rome*

The Thigh Baby

Under the Boardwalk

World's Biggest

Coming Soon

Backwoods Delivery - The Complete Daddy's Boy Series

Like the Greeks Do*

Higher Education*

Hoboes, Hustlers, and Jailbirds*

Small Cockpits and Big Hangars*

Tales of Two Daddies*

*Available as Paperbacks

Printed in the USA
CPSIA information can be obtained
at www.ICGtesting.com
CBHW051027180624
10202CB00006B/20

9 781963 667011